Defoe Abbott Marx Hardy Melville Montaigne Machiavelli Haggard Chesterton Cooper Emerson Joyce Austen Hugo Eliot Grimm
Stoker Carroll Christie Maupassant Byron Molière Schiller
Wilde Garnett Einstein Fitzgerald Hawthorne Smith Kafka Hall
Goethe Cotton Dostoyevsky
Baum Kipling Doyle Willis
Leslie Dumas Henry Nietzsche Balzac
Flaubert Turgenev Crane
Stockton Vatsyayana Verne
Burroughs Vinci
Curtis Tocqueville Gogol Busch
Homer Widger Tolstoy Whitman
Darwin Thoreau Twain Scott
Potter Freud Zola Lawrence Plato Harte
Kant Jowett Stevenson Dickens Hesse
Andersen Burton
London Descartes Cervantes Cooke
Poe Aristotle Wells Voltaire
Hale James Hastings
Bunner Shakespeare Irving
Richter Chambers
Doré Dante da Shaw Benedict Alcott
Swift Chekhov Pushkin
Wodehouse Newton

 tredition®

tredition was established in 2006 by Sandra Latusseck and Soenke Schulz. Based in Hamburg, Germany, tredition offers publishing solutions to authors and publishing houses, combined with world-wide distribution of printed and digital book content. tredition is uniquely positioned to enable authors and publishing houses to create books on their own terms and without conventional manu-facturing risks.

For more information please visit: www.tredition.com

TREDITION CLASSICS

This book is part of the TREDITION CLASSICS series. The creators of this series are united by passion for literature and driven by the intention of making all public domain books available in printed format again - worldwide. Most TREDITION CLASSICS titles have been out of print and off the bookstore shelves for decades. At tredition we believe that a great book never goes out of style and that its value is eternal. Several mostly non-profit literature projects provide content to tredition. To support their good work, tredition donates a portion of the proceeds from each sold copy. As a reader of a TREDITION CLASSICS book, you support our mission to save many of the amazing works of world literature from oblivion. See all available books at www.tredition.com.

Project Gutenberg

The content for this book has been graciously provided by Project Gutenberg. Project Gutenberg is a non-profit organization founded by Michael Hart in 1971 at the University of Illinois. The mission of Project Gutenberg is simple: To encourage the creation and distribution of eBooks. Project Gutenberg is the first and largest collection of public domain eBooks.

August First

Mary Raymond Shipman Andrews

Imprint

This book is part of TREDITION CLASSICS

Author: Mary Raymond Shipman Andrews
Cover design: Buchgut, Berlin – Germany

Publisher: tredition GmbH, Hamburg - Germany
ISBN: 978-3-8424-8713-0

www.tredition.com
www.tredition.de

"She—that's it—that's the gist of it—fool that I am."

(Page 101)

5

[Frontispiece: "She--that's it--that's the gist of it--fool that I am."]

AUGUST FIRST

"Whee!"

The long fingers pulled at the clerical collar as if they might tear it away. The alert figure swung across the room to the one window not wide open and the man pushed up the three inches possible. "Whee!" he brought out again, boyishly, and thrust away the dusty vines that hung against the opening from the stone walls of the parish house close by. He gasped; looked about as if in desperate need of relief; struck back the damp hair from his face. The heat was insufferable. In the west black-gray clouds rolled up like blankets, shutting out heaven and air; low thunder growled; at five o'clock of a midsummer afternoon it was almost dark; a storm was coming fast, and coolness would come with it, but in the meantime it was hard for a man who felt heat intensely just to get breath. His eyes stared at the open door of the room, down the corridor which led to the room, which turned and led by another open door to the street.

"If they're coming, why don't they come and get it over?" he murmured to himself; he was stifling — it was actual suffering.

He was troubled to-day, beyond this affliction of heat. He was the new curate of St. Andrew's, Geoffrey McBirney, only two months in the place — only two months, and here was the rector gone off for his summer vacation and McBirney left at the helm of the great city parish. Moreover, before the rector was gone a half-hour, here was the worst business of the day upon him, the hour between four and five when the rector was supposed to be found in the office, to receive any one who chose to come, for advice, for godly counsel, for "any old reason," as the man, only a few years out of college, put it to himself. He dreaded it; he dreaded it more than he did getting up into the pulpit of a Sunday and laying down the law — preaching. And he seriously wished that if any one was coming they would come now, and let him do his best, doggedly, as he meant to, and get them out of the way. Then he might go to work at things he understood. There was a funeral at seven; old Mrs. Harrow at the Home wanted to see him; and David Sterling had half promised to help him with St. Agnes's Mission School, and must be encouraged; a man in the worst tenement of the south city had raided his wife with a knife and there was trouble, physical and moral, and he must see to that; also Tommy Smith was dying at the Tuberculosis Hospital and had clung to his hands yesterday, and would not let him go—he must manage to get to little Tommy to-night. There was plenty of real work doing, so it did seem a pity to waste Lime waiting here for people who didn't come and who had, when they did come, only emotional troubles to air. And the heat—the unspeakable heat! "I can't stand it another second!" he burst out, aloud. "I'll die—I shall die!" He flung himself across the window-sill, with his head far out, trying to catch a breath of air that was alive.

As he stretched into the dim light, so, gasping, pulling again at the stiff collar, he was aware of a sound; he came back into the room with a spring; somebody was rapping at the open door. A young woman, in white clothes, with roses in her hat, stood there— refreshing as a cool breeze, he thought; with that, as if the thought, as if she, perhaps, had brought it, all at once there was a breeze; a heavenly, light touch on his forehead, a glorious, chilled current rushing about him.

"Thank Heaven!" he brought out involuntarily, and the girl, standing, facing him, looked surprised and, hesitating, stared at him. By that his dignity was on top.

"You wanted to see me?" he asked gravely. The girl flushed.

"No," she said, and stopped. He waited. "I didn't expect—" she began, and then he saw that she was very nervous. "I didn't expect—you."

He understood now. "You expected to find the rector. I'm sorry. He went off to-day for his vacation. I'm left in his place. Can I help you in any way?"

The girl stood uncertain, nervous, and said nothing. And looked at him, frightened, not knowing what to do. Then: "I wanted to see him—and now—it's you!" she stammered, and the man felt contrite that it was indubitably just himself. Contrite, then amused. But his look was steadily serious.

"I'm sorry," he said again. "If I would possibly do, I should be glad."

The girl burst into tears. That was bad. She dropped into a chair and sobbed uncontrollably, and he stood before her, and waited, and was uncomfortable. The sobbing stopped, and he had hopes, but the hat with roses was still plunged into the two bare hands—it was too hot for gloves. The thunder was nearer, muttering instant threatenings; the room was black; the air was heavy and cool like a wet cloth; the man in his black clothes stood before the white, collapsed figure in the chair and the girl began sobbing softly, wearily again.

"Please try to tell me." The young clergyman spoke quietly, in the detached voice which he had learned was best. "I can't do anything for you unless you tell me."

The top of the hat with roses seemed to pay attention; the flowers stopped bobbing; the sobs halted; in a minute a voice came. "I—know. I beg—your pardon. It was—such a shock to see—you." And then, most unexpectedly, she laughed. A wavering laugh that ended with a gasp—but laughter. "I'm not very civil. I meant just that—it wasn't you I expected. I was in church—ten days ago. And the rector said—people might come—here—and—he'd try to help them. It seemed to me I could talk to him. He was—fatherly. But you're"—the voice trailed into a sob—"young." A laugh was due here, he thought, but none came. "I mean—it's harder."

"I understand," he spoke quietly. "You would feel that way. And there's no one like the rector—one could tell him anything. I know that. But if I can help you—I'm here for that, you know. That's all there is to consider." The impersonal, gentle interest had instant effect.

"Thank you," she said, and with a visible effort pulled herself together, and rose and stood a moment, swaying, as it an inward indecision blew her this way and that. With that a great thunder-clap close by shook heaven and earth and drowned small human voices, and the two in the dark office faced each other waiting Nature's good time. As the rolling echoes died away, "I think I had better wait to see the rector," she said, and held out her hand. "Thank you for your kindness—and patience. I am—I am—in a good deal of

trouble—" and her voice shook, in spite of her effort. Suddenly—
"I'm going to tell you," she said. "I'm going to ask you to help me, if
you will be so good. You are here for the rector, aren't you?"

"I am here for the rector," McBirney answered gravely. "I wish to
do all I can for—any one."

She drew a long sigh of comfort. "That's good—that's what I
want," she considered aloud, and sat down once more. And the man
lifted a chair to the window where the breeze reached him. Rain
was falling now in sheets and the steely light played on his dark
face and sombre dress and the sharp white note of his collar.
Through the constant rush and patter of the rain the girl's voice
went on—a low voice with a note of pleasure and laughter in it
which muted with the tragedy of what she said.

"I'm thinking of killing myself," she began, and the eyes of the
man widened, but he did not speak. "But I'm afraid of what comes
after. They tell you that it's everlasting torment—but I don't believe
it. Parsons mostly tell you that. The fear has kept me from doing it.
So when I heard the rector in church two weeks ago, I felt as if he'd
be honest—and as if he might know—as much as any one can
know. He seemed real to me, and clever—I thought it would help if
I could talk to him—and I thought maybe I could trust him to tell
me honestly—in confidence, you know—if he really and truly
thought it was wrong for a person to kill herself. I can't see why."
She glanced at the attentive, quiet figure at the window. "Do you
think so?" she asked. He looked at her, but did not speak. She went
on. "Why is it wrong? They say God gives life and only God should
take it away. Why? It's given—we don't ask for it, and no conditions
come with it. Why should one, if it gets unendurable, keep an un-
asked, unwanted gift? If somebody put a ball of bright metal into
your hands and it was pretty at first and nice to play with, and then
turned red-hot, and hurt, wouldn't it be silly to go on holding it? I
don't know much about God, anyway," she went on a bit forlornly;
not irreverently, but as if pain had burned off the shell of conventions and reserves of every day, and actual facts lay bare. "I don't
feel as if He were especially real—and the case I'm in is awfully real.
I don't know if He would mind my killing myself—and if He
would, wouldn't He understand I just have to? If He's really good?

But then, if He was angry, might He punish me forever, afterward?" She drew her shoulders together with a frightened, childish movement. "I'm afraid of forever," she said.

The rain beat in noisily against the parish house wall; the wet vines flung about wildly; a floating end blew in at the window and the young man lifted it carefully and put it outside again. Then, "Can you tell me why you want to kill yourself?" he asked, and his manner, free from criticism or disapproval, seemed to quiet her.

"Yes. I want to tell you. I came here to tell the rector." The grave eyes of the man, eyes whose clearness and youth seemed to be such an age-old youth and clearness as one sees in the eyes of the sibyls in the frescoes of the Sistine Chapel—eyes empty of a thought of self, impersonal, serene with the serenity of a large atmosphere— the unflinching eyes of the man gazed at the girl as she talked.

She talked rapidly, eagerly, as if each word lifted pressure. "It's this way—I'm ill—hopelessly ill. Yes—it's absolutely so. I've got to die. Two doctors said so. But I'll live—maybe five years—possibly ten. I'm twenty-three now—and I may live ten years. But if I do that—if I live five years even—most of it will be as a helpless invalid—I'll have to get stiff, you know." There was a rather dreadful levity in the way she put it. "Stiffer and stiffer—till I harden into one position, sitting or lying down, immovable. I'll have to go on living that way—years, you see. I'll have to choose which way. Isn't it hideous? And I'll go on living that way, you see. Me. You don't know, of course, but it seems particularly hideous, because I'm not a bit an immovable sort. I ride and play tennis and dance, all those things, more than most people. I care about them—a lot." One could see it in the vivid pose of the figure. "And, you know, it's really too much to expect. I *won't* stiffen gently into a live corpse. No!" The sliding, clear voice was low, but the "no" meant itself.

From the quiet figure by the window came no response; the girl could see the man's face only indistinctly in the dim, storm-washed light; receding thunder growled now and again and the noise of the rain came in soft, fierce waves; at times, lightning flashed a weird clearness over the details of the room and left them vaguer.

"Why don't you say something?" the girl threw at him. "What do you think? Say it."

"Are you going to tell me the rest?" the man asked quietly.

"The rest? Isn't that enough? What makes you think there's more?" she gasped.

"I don't know what makes me. I do. Something in your manner, I suppose. You mustn't tell me if you wish not, but I'd be able to help you better if I knew everything. As long as you've told me so much."

There was a long stillness in the dim room; the dashing rain and the muttering thunder were the only sounds in the world. The white dress was motionless in the chair, vague, impersonal—he could see only the blurred suggestion of a face above it; it got to be fantastic, a dream, a condensation of the summer lightning and the storm-clouds; unrealities seized the quick imagination of the man; into his fancy came the low, buoyant voice out of key with the words.

"Yes, there's more. A love story, of course—there's always that. Only this is more an un-love story, as far as I'm in it." She stopped again. "I don't know why I should tell you this part."

"Don't, if you don't want to," the man answered promptly, a bit coldly. He felt a clear distaste for this emotional business; he would much prefer to "cut it out," as he would have expressed it to himself.

"I *do* want to—now. I didn't mean to. But it's a relief." And it came to him sharply that if he was to be a surgeon of souls, what business had he to shrink from blood?

"I am here to relieve you if I can. It's what I most wish to do—for any one," he said gently then. And the girl suddenly laughed again.

"For any one," she repeated. "I like it that way." Her eyes, wandering a moment about the dim, bare office, rested on a calendar in huge lettering hanging on the wall, rested on the figures of the date of the day. "I want to be just a number, a date—August first—I'm that, and that's all. I'll never see you again, I hope. But you are good and I'll be grateful. Here's the way things are. Three years ago I got engaged to a man. I suppose I thought I cared about him. I'm a fool. I get—fads." A short, soft laugh cut the words. "I got about that over the man. He fascinated me. I thought it was—more. So I got engaged to him. He was a lot of things he oughtn't to be; my people objected. Then, later, my father was ill—dying. He asked me to break it off, and I did—he'd been father and mother both to me, you see. But I still thought I cared. I hadn't seen the man much. My father died, and then I heard about the man, that he had lost money and been ill and that everybody was down on him; he drank, you know, and got into trouble. So I just felt desperate; I felt it was my fault, and that there was nobody to stand by him. I felt as if I could pull him up and make his life over—pretty conceited of me, I expect—but I felt that. So I wrote him a letter, six months ago, out of a blue sky, and told him that if he wanted me still he could have me. And he did. And then I went out to live with my uncle, and this man lives in that town too, and I've seen him ever since, all the time. I know him now. And—" Out of the dimness the clergyman felt, rather than saw, a smile widen—child-like, sardonic—a curious, contagious smile, which bewildered him, almost made him smile back. "You'll think me a pitiful person," she went on, "and I am. But I—almost—hate him. I've promised to marry him and I can't bear to have his fingers touch me."

In Geoffrey McBirney's short experience there had been nothing which threw a light on what he should do with a situation of this sort. He was keenly uncomfortable; he wished the rector had stayed at home. At all events, silence was safe, so he was silent with all his might.

"When the doctors told me about my malady a month ago, the one light in the blackness was that now I might break my engagement, and I hurried to do it. But he wouldn't. He—" A sound came, half laugh, half sob. "He's certainly faithful. But—I've got a lot of money. It's frightful," she burst forth. "It's the crowning touch, to doubt even his sincerity. And I may be wrong—he may care for me. He says so. I think my heart has ossified first, and is finished, for it is quite cold when he says so. I *can't* marry him! So I might as well kill myself," she concluded, in a casual tone, like a splash of cold water on the hot intensity of the sentences before. And the man, listening, realized that now he must say something. But what to say? His mind seemed blank, or at best a muddle of protest. And the light-hearted voice spoke again. "I think I'll do it to-night, unless you tell me I'd certainly go to hell forever."

Then the protest was no longer muddled, but defined. "You mustn't do that," he said, with authority. "Suppose a man is riding a runaway horse and he loses his nerve and throws himself off and is killed—is that as good a way as if he sat tight and fought hard until the horse ran into a wall and killed him? I think not. And besides, any second, his pull on the reins may tell, and the horse may slow down, and his life may be saved. It's better riding and it's better living not to give in till you're thrown. Your case looks hopeless to you, but doctors have been wrong plenty of times; diseases take unexpected turns; you may get well."

"Then I'd have to marry *him*," she interrupted swiftly.

"You ought not to marry him if you dislike him"—and the young parson felt himself flush hotly, and was thankful for the darkness; what a fool a fellow felt, giving advice about a love-affair!

"I *have* to. You see—he's pathetic. He'd go back into the depths if I let go, and—and I'm fond of him, in a way."

"Oh!"—the masculine mind was bewildered. "I understood that you—disliked him."

"Why, I do. But I'm just fond of him." Then she laughed again. "Any woman would know how I mean it. I mean—I am fond of him—I'd do anything for him. But I don't believe in him, and the thought of—of marrying him makes me desperate."

"Then you should not."

"I have to, if I live. So I'm going to kill myself to-night. You have nothing to say against it. You've said nothing—that counts. If you said I'd certainly go to hell, I might not—but you don't say that. I think you can't say it." She stood up. "Thank you for listening patiently. At least you have helped me to come to my decision. I'm going to. To-night."

This was too awful. He had helped her to decide to kill herself. He could not let her go that way. He stood before her and talked with all his might. "You cannot do that. You must not. You are over-strained and excited, and it is no time to do an irrevocable thing. You must wait till you see things calmly, at least. Taking your own life is not a thing to decide on as you might decide on going to a ball. How do you know that you will not be bitterly sorry to-morrow if you do that to-night? It's throwing away the one chance a person has to make the world better and happier. That's what you're here for—not to enjoy yourself."

She put a quiet sentence, in that oddly buoyant voice, into the stream of his words. "Still, you don't say I'd go to hell forever," she commented.

"Is that your only thought?" he demanded indignantly. "Can't you think of what's brave and worth while—of what's decent for a big thing like a soul? A soul that's going on living to eternity—do you want to blacken that at the start? Can't you forget your little moods and your despair of the moment?"

"No, I can't." The roses bobbed as she shook her head. The man, in his heart, knew how it was, and did not wonder. But he must some-how stop this determination which he had—she said—helped to form. A thought came to him; he hesitated a moment, and then broke out impetuously: "Let me do this—let me write to you; I'm not saying things straight. It's hard. I think I could write more clear-ly. And it's unfair not to give me a hearing. Will you promise only this, not to do it till you've read my letter?"

Slowly the youth, the indomitable brightness in the girl forged to the front. She looked at him with the dawn of a smile in her eyes, and he saw all at once, with a passing vision, that her eyes were very blue and that her hair was bright and light—a face vivid and responsive.

"Why, yes. There's no particular reason for to-night. I can wait. But I'm going home to-morrow, to my uncle's place at Forest Gate. I'll never be here again. The people I'm with are going away to live next month. I'll never see you again. You don't know my name." She considered a moment. "I'd rather not have you know it. You may write to—" She laughed. "I said I was just a date—you may write to August First, Forest Gate, Illinois. Say care of, care of—" Again she laughed. "Oh, well, care of Robert Halarkenden. That will reach me."

Quite gravely the man wrote down the fantastic address. "Thank you. I will write at once. You promised?"

"Yes." She put out her hand. "You've been very good to me. I shall never see you again. Good-by."

"Good-by," he said, and the room was suddenly so still, so empty, so dark that it oppressed him.

WARCHESTER,
  St. Andrew's Parish House,
    August 5th.

This is to redeem my promise. When we talked that afternoon, it seemed to me that I should be able to write the words I could not say. Every day since then I have said "Tomorrow I shall be able to tell her clearly." The clearness has not come—that's why I have put it off. It hasn't yet come. Sometimes—twice, I think—I have seen it all plainly. Just for a second—in a sort of flash. And then it dropped back into this confusion.

I won't insult you by attempting to discount your difficulties. You have worked out for yourself a calculation made, at one time or another, by many more people than you would imagine. And your answer is wrong. I know that. You know it too. When you say that you are afraid of what may come after, you admit that what you intend to do is impossible. If you were not convinced of something after, you would go on and do what you propose. Which shows that there is an error in your mathematics. Do you at all know what I mean?

I must make you understand. I can see why you find the prospect unendurable. You don't look far enough, that is all. Why do people shut themselves up in the air-tight box of a possible three score years and ten, and call it life? How can you, who are so alive, do so? It seems that you have fallen into the strangely popular error of thinking that clocks measure life. That is not what they are for. A clock is the contrivance of springs and wheels whereby the ambitious, early of a summer's day when sane people are asleep or hunting flowers on the hill-side, keep tally of the sun. Those early on the hill-side see the gray lighten and watch it flush to rose—the advent of the day-spring—and go on picking flowers. They of the clocks are one day older—these have seen a sunrise. There is the difference.

If you really thought that all there is to life is that part of it we have here in this world—if you believed that—then what you contemplate doing would be nothing worse than unsportsmanlike. But you do not believe that. You are afraid of what might come—after. You came to me—or you came to the rector—in the hope of being assured that your fear was groundless. You had a human desire for the advice of a "professional." You still wish that assurance—that is why you promised to wait for this letter. You told me your case; you wanted expert testimony. Here it is: You need not be afraid. God will not be angry—God will not punish you. You said that you did not know much about God. Surely you know this much—anger can never be one of His attributes. God is never angry. Men would be angry if they were treated as they treat Him—that is all. In mathematics, certain letters represent certain unknown quantities. So words are only the symbols for imperfectly realized ideas. If by "hell" you understand what that word means to me—the endlessness of life with nothing in it that makes life worth while—then, if you still want my opinion, I think that you will most certainly go there. God will not be angry. God will not send you there, you will have sent yourself—it will not be God's punishment laid on you, it will be your punishment laid by you on yourself. But it is not in you to let that come to pass.

All of the "philosophies of life," as they are called, are, I think, varieties of two. I suppose Materialism and Idealism cover them. Those who hold with the first are in the air-tight box of years and call it life. The others are in the box, too, but they call it time. And they know that, after all, the box is really not air-tight; each of them remembers the day when he first discovered that there were cracks in the box, and the day he learned that one could best see through those narrow openings by coming up resolutely to the hard necessary walls that hold one in. Then came the astounding enlightenment that only a shred of reality was within the cramped prison of the box—just a darkened, dusty bit—that all the beautiful rest of it lay outside. These are the ones who, pressing up against the rough walls of the box, see, through their chinks, the splendor of what lies outside—see it and know that, one day, they shall have it.

The others, the Materialists, never come near the walls of the box, except to bang their heads. Their reality is inside. These call life a thing. The Idealists know that it is a process, and there is not a tree or a flower or a blade of grass or a road-side weed but proves them right. It is a process, and the end of it is perfection—nothing less. The perfection of the physical is approximated to here in this world, and, after that, the tired hands are folded, and the worn-out body laid away. But even the very saints of God barely touch, here, the edges of the possible perfection of the soul. Why, it is that that lifts us—that possibility of going on and on—out of imaginable bounds, into glory after glory—until the wisdom of the ages is foolishness and time has no meaning where, in the reaches of eternity, the climbing soul thinks with the mind of God.

You were going to cut yourself off from that! At the very start, you were going to fling away your single glorious chance—you, who told me that in less than ten of these littlenesses called "years" you might be allowed to go out into a larger place. Remember, you can't kill your soul. But, because you have been trusted with personality you can, if you wish, show an unforgiveable contempt for your beginning life. But, if you do that—if you treat your single opportunity like that—can you believe that another will be given you?

You cannot do this thing. I say to you that there are openings in the box. Find a fissure in the rough wall. Then, look! This isn't life—only the smallest bit of it. The rest is outside. It is not a question of God—it is not a question of punishment. It is this—what are *you* going to do with your soul?

I wonder if you have read as far as this. I wonder if I have been at all intelligible?

Will Robert Halarkenden see that you get this thick letter? There is only one way by which I can know that it found you.

I know that I have been hopelessly inadequate—perhaps grotesque. To see it and be unable to tell you—imagine the awfulness! Give me another chance. I was not going to ask that, but I must. Can't you see I've got to show you? I mean—about another chance—will you not renew that promise? Will you not send a word in answer to this letter, and promise once more not to do anything decisive until you have heard from me again? I am

Sincerely yours,
  GEOFFREY McBIRNEY.

FOREST GATE, August 8th.

MY DEAR MR. McBIRNEY —

Robert Halarkenden saw that I got it. You don't know who Robert Halarkenden is, do you? He's interesting, and likely you never will know about him — but it doesn't matter. Your letter left me with a curious feeling, a feeling which I think I used to have as a child when I was just waking from one of the strong dreams of childhood which "trail clouds of glory." It was a feeling that I had been swept off my feet and made to use my wings — only I haven't much in the line of wings. But it was as if you had lifted me into an atmosphere where I gasped — and used wings. It was grand, but startling and difficult, and I can't fly. I flopped down promptly and began crawling about on the ground busily. Yet the "cloud of glory" has trailed a bit, through the gray days since. I don't mind telling you that I locked the letter in the drawer with a shiny little pistol I have had for some time, so that I can't get to the pistol without seeing the letter. I'm playing this game with you very fairly, you see — which sounds conceited and as if the game meant anything to you, a stranger. But because you are good, and saving souls is your job, and because you think my soul might get wrecked, for those reasons it does mean a little I think.

About your letter. Some of it is wonderful. I never thought about it that way. In a conventional, indifferent fashion I've believed that if I'm good I'll go to a place called heaven when I die. It hasn't interested me very much — what I've heard has sounded rather dull — the people supposed to be on the express trains there have, many of them, been people I didn't want to play with. I've cared to be straight and broad-minded and all that because I naturally object to sneaks and catty people — not for much other reason. But this is a wonderful idea of yours, that my only life — as I've regarded it — is just about five minutes anyhow, of a day that goes on from strength to strength. You've somehow put an atmosphere into it, and a reality. I believe you believe it. Excuse me — I'm not being flippant; I'm only being deadly real. I may shoot myself tonight; tomorrow morning I may be dead, whatever that means. Anyhow, I haven't a desire to talk etiquettically about things like this. And I won't, whatever you may think of me. Your letter didn't convince me. It inspired me; it made me feel that maybe—just maybe—it might be worth while to wiggle painfully, or more painfully lie still in your "box" and that I'd come out—all of us poor things would come out—into gloriousness some time. I would hate to have queered myself, you know, by going off at half-cock. But would it queer me? What do you know about it? How can you tell? I might be put back a few laps—I'm not being flippant, I simply don't know how to say it—and then, anyhow, I'd be outside the "box," wouldn't I? And in the freedom—and I could catch up, maybe. Yet, it might be the other way; I might have shown an "unforgiveable contempt" for my life. Unforgiveable—by whom? You say God forgives forever—well, I know He must, if He's a God worth worshipping. So I don't know what you mean by "unforgiveable." And you don't know if it's my "single, glorious chance" at life. How can you know? On the other hand, I don't know but that it is—that's the risk, I suppose—and it is a hideous risk. I suppose likely you mean that. You see, when it gets down below Sunday-school lessons and tradition, I don't know much what I do believe. I'd rather believe in God because everything seems to fly to pieces in an uncomfortable way if one doesn't. But is that any belief? As to "faith," that sounds rather nonsense to me. What on earth is faith if it isn't shutting your eyes and playing you believe what you really don't believe? Likely I'm an idiot—I suspect that—but I'd gladly have it proved. And here I am away off from the point and arguing about huge things that I can't even see across, much less handle. I beg your pardon; I beg your pardon for all the time I'm taking and the bother I'm making. Still, I'm going on living till I get your next letter—I promise, as you ask. I'm glad to promise because of the first letter, and of the glimpse down a vista, and the breath of strange, fresh air it seemed to bring. I have an idea that I stumbled on rather a wonderful person that day I missed the rector. Or is it possibly just the real belief in a wonderful thing that shines through you? But then, you're clever besides; I'm clever enough to know that. Only, don't digress so; don't write a lot of lovely English about clocks and getting up early. That's not to the point. That irritates me. I suppose it's because you see things covered with sunlight and wonder, and you just have to tell about it as you go along. All right, if you must. But if you digress too much, I'll go and shoot, and that will finish the correspondence.

Indeed I know that this is a most extraordinary and unconventional letter to send a man whom I have seen once. But you are not human to me; you are a spirit of the thunder-storm of August first. I cannot even remember how you look. Your voice — I'd recognize that. It has a quality of — what is it? Atmosphere, vibration, purity, roundness — no, I can't get it. You see I may be unconventional, I may be impertinent, I may be personal, because I am not a person, only

    Yours gratefully,
      AUGUST FIRST.

FOREST GATE, August 10th.

MY DEAR MR. MCBIRNEY —

This is just a word to tell you that you must answer rather quickly, or I might not keep my promise. Last night I was frightened; I had a hideous evening. Alec was here — the man I'm to marry if nothing saves me — and it was bad. He won't release me, and I won't break my word unless he does. And after he was gone I went through a queer time; I think a novel would call it an obsession. Almost without my will, almost as if I were another person, I tried to get the pistol. And your letter guarded it. My first personality *couldn't* lift your letter off to get the pistol. Did you hypnotize me? It's like the queer things one reads in psychological books. I *couldn't* get past that letter. Of course, I'm in some strained, abnormal condition, and that's all, but send me another letter, for if one is a barricade two should be a fortress. And I nearly broke down the barricade; Number Two did, that is.

Is it hot in Warchester? It is so heavenly here this morning that I wish I could send you a slice of it — coolness and birds singing and trees rustling. I think of you going up and down tenement stairs in the heat — and I know you hate heat — I took that in. This house stands in big grounds and the lake, seventy-five miles long, you know, roars up on the beach below it. I wish I could send you a slice. Write me, please — and you so busy! I am a selfish person.

AUGUST FIRST.

WARCHESTER,
   St. Andrew's Parish House,
      August 12th.

Yesterday it rained. And then the telephone rang, and some incoherent person mumbled an address out in the furthest suburb. It was North Baxter Court. You never saw that—a row of yellow houses with the door-sills level to the mud and ashes of the alley, and swarms of children who stare and whisper, "Here's the 'Father.'" Number 7 1/2 was marked with a membraneous croup sign—the usual lie to avoid strict quarantine and still get anti-toxin at the free dispensary; the room was unspeakable—shut windows and a crowd of people. A woman, young, sat rocking back and forth, half smothering a baby in her arms. Nobody spoke. It took time to get the windows open and persuade the woman to lay the child on the bed in the corner. There wasn't anything else to use, so I fanned the baby with my straw hat—until, finally, it got away from North Baxter Court forever. Which was as it should be. Then tumult. Probably you are not in a position to know that few spectacles are more hideous than the unrestrained grief of the poor. The things they said and did—it was unhuman, indecent. I can't describe it. As I was leaving, after a pretty bad half hour, I met the doctor at the door—one of these half-drunken quacks who live on the ignorant. That child died of diphtheria. I knew it, and he admitted it. The funeral was this breathless morning, with details that may not be written down.

   LATER.

Somebody interrupted. And now it's long past midnight. I must try to send you some answer to your letter. I have been thinking—the combination may strike you as odd—of North Baxter Court and you. Not that the happenings of yesterday were unusual. That is just it—they come almost every day, things like that. And you, with your birds and rustling trees and your lake—you keep a shiny pistol in the drawer of your dressing-table, and write me the sort of letter that came from you this morning. When all these people need *you*— these blind, dumb animals, stumbling through the sordid, hopeless years—need you, because, in spite of everything, you are still so much further along than they, because you are capable of seeing where their eyes are shut, because you and your kind can help them, and put the germ of life into the deadness of their days, because of all that makes you what you are, and gives you the chance to become infinitely more—you, in the face of all that, can sit down in the fragrance of a garden-scented breeze and write as you have done about God and the things that matter.

You said that it was not flippancy. Your whole point of view is wrong. Do not ask me how I "know"—some conclusions do not need to be analyzed. I wonder if you realize, for instance, what you said about faith? I haven't the charity to call it even childish. Have you ever got below the surface of anything at all? Do you want to know what it is that has brought you to the verge of suicide? It is not your horror of illness, nor your oddly concluded determination to marry a man whom you do not love. Suicide is an ugly word—I notice that you avoid it—and love is a big word; I am using them understandingly and soberly. You came to the edge of this thing for the reason that there is not an element of bigness in your life, and there never has been. You lack the balance of large ideas. This man of whom you tell me—of course you do not love him—you have not yet the capacity for understanding the meaning of the word. You like to ride and you like to dance and you are fond of the things that please, but you do not love anybody or even any thing. You are living, yes, but you are asleep. And it is because you are ignorant.

If your letter had been designedly flippant, it would merely have annoyed. It is the unconscious flippancy in it that is so discouraging. You do not know what you believe because you believe nothing. Your most coherent conception of God is likely a hazy vision of a majestic figure seated on a cloud—a long-bearded patriarch, wearing a golden crown—the composite of famous pictures that you have seen. You have been taught to believe in a personal God, and you have never taken the trouble to get beyond the notion that personality—God's or anybody's—is mainly a matter of the possession of such things as hands and feet. What can be the meaning to one like you of the truth that we are made in the image of God? The Kingdom of Heaven—that whole whirling activity of the commonwealth of God—the citizenship towards which you might be pointing Baxter Court—you have not even imagined it. I am not being sentimental. Don't misunderstand. Don't fancy, for instance, that I am exhorting you to go slumming. Deliberately or not, you took a wrong impression from my first letter. You can't mistake this. Reach after a few of the realities. Why not shut your questioning mind a while and open your soul? *Live* a little—begin to realize that there is a world outside yourself. Try to get beyond the view-point of a child. And, if I have not angered you beyond words, let me know how you get on.

The unconventionality of this correspondence, you see, is not all on one side. If you found English to your taste in what I wrote before, this time you have plain truths, perhaps less satisfactory. You are not in a position to decide some matters. I do not ask you to let me decide them for you. I have only tried to indicate some reasons why you must wait before you act. And I think it has made you angry. One has to risk that. Yesterday I could not have imagined sending a letter like this to anybody. But it goes—and to you. I ask you to answer it. I think you owe me that. It hasn't been exactly easy to write.

One more thing—don't trust letters to stand between you and the toy in the dressing-table drawer. Any barrier there, to be in the least effective, will have to be of your own building.

GEOFFREY McBIRNEY.

About a month after the above letter had been received, on September 10th, Geoffrey McBirney, dashing down the three flights of stairs in the Parish House from his quarters on the top floor, peered into the letter-box on the way to morning service. He peered eagerly. There had been no answer to his letter; it was a month; he was surprisingly uneasy. But there was nothing in the mail-box, so he swept along to the vestry-room, and got into his cassock and read service to the handful of people in the chapel, with a sense of sick depression which he manfully choked down at every upheaval, but which was distinctly there quite the same. Service over, there were things to be done for three hours; also there was to be a meeting in his rooms at twelve o'clock to consider the establishment of a new mission, his special interest, in the rough country at the west of the city; the rector and the bishop and two others were coming. He hurried home and up to his place, at eleven-forty-five, and gave a hasty look about to see if things were fairly proper for august people. Not that the bishop would notice. He dusted off the library table with his handkerchief, put one book discreetly on the back side of the table instead of in front, swept an untidy box of cigarettes into a drawer, and gathered up the fresh pile of wash from a chair and put it on the bed in his sleeping-room and shut the door hard. Then he gazed about with the air of a satisfied housekeeper. He lifted up a loudly ticking clock which would not go except lying on its face, and regarded it. Five minutes to twelve, and they were sure to be late. He extracted a cigarette from the drawer and lighted it; his thoughts, loosened from immediate pressure, came back slowly, surely, to the empty mailbox, his last letter, the girl whom he knew grotesquely as "August First." Why had she not written for four weeks? He had considered that question from many angles for about three weeks, and the question rose and confronted him, always new, at each leisure moment. It was disproportionate, it showed lack of balance, that it should loom so large on the horizon, with the hundred other interests, tragedies, which were there for him; but it loomed.

Why had he written her that hammer-and-tongs answer? he demanded of himself, not for the first time. Of course, it was true, but when one is drowning, one does not want reams of truth, one wants a rope. He had stood on the shore and lectured the girl, ordered her to strike out and swim for it, and not be so criminally selfish as to drop into the ocean; that was what he had done. And the girl—what had she done? Heaven only knew. Probably gone under. It looked more so each day. Why could he not have been gentler, even if she was undeveloped, narrow, asleep? Because she was rich—he answered his own question to himself—because he had no belief in rich people; only a hard distrust of whatever they did. That was wrong; he knew it. He blew a cloud of smoke to the ceiling and spoke aloud, impatiently. "All the same, they're none of them any good," said Geoffrey McBirney, and directed himself to stop worrying about this thing. And with that came a sudden memory of a buoyant, fresh voice saying tremendous words like a gentle child, of the blue flash of eyes only half seen in a storm-swept darkness, of roses bobbing.

McBirney flung the half-smoked cigarette into the fireplace and lifted the neurotic clock: twelve-twenty. The postman came again at twelve. He would risk the rector and the bishop. Down the stairs he plunged again and brought up at the mail-box. There was a letter. Hurriedly, he snatched it out and turned the address up; a miracle—it was from the girl. The street door darkened; McBirney looked up. The rector and the bishop were coming in, the others at their heels. He thrust the envelope into his pocket, his pulse beating distinctly faster, and turned to meet his guests.

When at three o'clock he got back to his quarters, after an exciting meeting of an hour, after lunch at the rectory, after seeing the bishop off on the 2.45 to New York, he locked his door first, and then hurriedly drew out the letter lying all this time unread. He tore untidily at the flap, and with that suddenly he stopped, and the luminous eyes took on an odd, sarcastic expression. "What a fool!" he spoke, half aloud, and put the letter down and strolled across the room and gazed out of the window. "What an ass! I'm allowing myself to get personally interested in this case; or to imagine that I'm personally interested. Folly. The girl is nothing to me. I'll never see her again. I care about her as I would about anybody in trouble. And—that's all. This lunacy of restlessness over the situation has got—to—stop." He was firm with himself. He sat down at his table and wrote a business note before he touched the letter again; but he saw the letter out of the tail of his eye all the time and he knew his pulse was going harder as, finally, he lifted the torn envelope with elaborate carelessness, and drew out the sheets of writing.

My dear Mr. McBirney [the girl began], did anybody ever tell a story about a big general who limbered up his artillery, if that's the thing they do, and shouted orders, and cracked whips and rattled wheels and went through evolutions, and finally, with thunder and energy, trained a huge Krupp gun—or something—on a chipmunk? If there is such a story, and you've heard it, doesn't it remind you of your last letter at me? Not to me, I mean *at* me. It was a wonderful letter again, but when I got through I had a feeling that what I needed was not suicide—I do dare say the word, you see—but execution. Maybe shooting is too good for me. And you know I appreciate every minute how unnecessary it is for you to bother with me, and to put your time and your strength, both of which mean much to many people, into hammering me. And how good you are to do that. I am worthless, as you say between every two lines. Yet I'm a soul—you say that too, and so on a par with those tragic souls in North Baxter Court. Only, I feel that you have no patience with me for getting underfoot when you're on your way to big issues. But do have patience, please—it means as much to me as to anybody in your tenements. I'm far down, and I'm struggling for breath, and there seems to be no land in sight, nothing to hold to except you. I'm sorry if you dislike to have it so, but it is so; your letters mean anchorage. I'd blow out to sea if I didn't have them to hope for. You ought to be glad of that; you're doing good, even if it is only to a flippant, shallow, undeveloped doll. I can call myself names—oh yes.

I have been slow answering, though likely you haven't noticed [McBirney smiled queerly], because I have been doing a thing. You said you didn't advise me to go slumming—though I think you did—what else? You said I ought to get beyond the view-point of a child; to realize the world outside myself.

I sat down, and in my limited way—I mean that, sincerely, humbly—I considered what I could do. No slumming—and, in any case, there's none to be done in Forest Gate. So I thought I'd better clear my vision with great books. I went to Robert Halarkenden, the only bookish person in my surroundings, and asked him about it—about what would open up a larger horizon for me. And he, not understanding much what I was at, recommended two or three things which I have been and am reading. I thought I'd try to be a little more intelligent at least before I answered your letter. Don't thunder at me—I'm stumbling about, trying to get somewhere. I've read some William James and some John Fiske, and I realize this—that I did more or less think God was a very large, stately old man. An "anthropomorphic deity." Fiske says that is the God of the lower peoples; that was my God. Also I realize this—that, somehow, some God, *the* God if I can get to Him, might help might be my only chance. What do you think? Is this any better? Is it any step? If it is, it's a very precarious one, for though it thrills me to my bones sometimes to think that a real power might lift me and bring me through, if I just ask Him, yet sometimes all that hope goes and I drop in a heap mentally with no starch in me, no grip to try to hold to any idea—just a heap of tired, dull mind and nerves, and for my only desire that subtle, pushing desire to end it all quickly. Once an odd thing happened. When I was collapsed like that, just existing, suddenly there was a feeling, a brand-new feeling of letting go of the old rubbish that was and somebody else pervading it through and through and taking all the responsibility. And I held on tight, something as I do to your letters, and the first thing, I was believing that help was coming—and help came. That was the best day I've had since I saw those devil doctors. Do you suppose that was faith? Where did it come from? I'd been praying—but awfully queer prayers; I said "Oh just put me through somehow; give me what I need; *I* don't know what it is; how can you expect me to—I'm a worm." I suppose that was irreverent, but I can't help it. It was all I could say. And that came, whatever it was. Do you suppose it was an answer to my blind, gasping prayer?

Now I'm going to ask you to do a thing—but don't if it's the least bother. I don't want you to talk to me about myself just now, any more. And I want to hear more about North Baxter Court and such. You don't know how that stirred me. What a worth-while life you lead, doing actual, life-and-death things for people who bitterly need things done. It seems to me glorious. I could give up everything to feel a stream of genuine living through me such as you have, all your rushing days. Yes—I could—but yet, maybe I wouldn't make good. But I do care for "life, and life more abundantly," and the only way of getting it that I've known has been higher fences to jump, and more dances and better tennis and such. I never once realized the way you get it—my! what a big way. And how heavenly it must be to give hope and health and help to people. I adore sending the maids out in the car, or giving them my clothes. I just selfishly like pleasing people, and I think giving is the best amusement extant—and you give your very self from morning to night. You lucky person! How could I do that? Could I? Would I balk, do you think? You say I'm not capable of loving anything or anybody. I think you are wrong. I think I could, some day, love somebody as hard as any woman or man has, ever. Not Alec. What will happen if I marry Alec and then do that—if the somebody comes? That would be a mess; the worst mess yet. The end of the world; but I forget; my world ends anyhow. I'll be a stone image in a chair—a cold, unloveable stone image with a hot, boiling heart. I won't—I *won't*. This world is just five minutes, maybe—but me—in a chair—ten years. Oh—I *won't*.

What I want you to do is to write me just about the things you're doing, and the people—the poor people, and the pitiful things and the funny things—the atmosphere of it. Could you forget that you don't know me, and write as you would to a cousin or an old friend? That would be good. That would help. Only, anyhow, write, for without your letters I can't tell what bomb may burst. Don't thunder next time. But even if you thunder, write. The letters do guard the pistol—I can't help it if you say not. It has to be so now, anyway. They guard it. Always—

AUGUST FIRST.

WARCHESTER,
St. Andrew's Parish House,
Sept. 12th.

You're right. It's idiotic to leap on people like that. I knew I was all wrong the moment after the letter went. And when nothing came from you—it wasn't pleasant. I nearly wrote—I more nearly telegraphed your Robert Halarkenden. Do you mind if I say that for two days, just lately—in fact, they were yesterday and the day before—I was on the edge of asking for leave of absence to go west? You see, if you had done it, it was so plainly my fault. And I had to know. Then I argued—it's ghastly, but I argued that it would be in the papers. And it wasn't. Of course, it might possibly have been kept out. But generally it isn't. My knowledge of happenings in Chicago and thereabouts, since my last letter, would probably surprise you a little. Yes, I "noticed" that you didn't write—more than I noticed the heat, which, now I think, has been bad. But when you're pretty sure you've blundered in a matter of life and death, you don't pray for rain.

You've turned a corner. A corner. *The* corner—the big one, is further along, and then there's the hill and the hot sun on the dusty road. You'll need your sporting instincts. But you've got them. So had St. Paul and those others who furnished the groundwork for that oft-mentioned Roman holiday. That's religion, as I see it. That's what *they* did; pushed on—faced things down—went out smiling— "gentlemen unafraid." It's like swimming—you can't go under if you make the least effort. That's the law—of physics and, therefore, of God. The experience you tell of is exactly what you have the right to expect. The prayer you said; that's the only way to come at it, your-self—talking—with that Other. There's a poem—you know—the man who "caught at God's skirts and prayed."

But you said not to write about you. All right then, I've been to the theatre, the one at the end of our block. That may strike you as tame. But you don't know Mrs. Jameson. She's the relict of the late senior warden. A disapproving party, trimmed with jet beads and a lorgnette. A few days after the rector left me in charge she tri-umphed into the office, rattled the beads and got behind the lor-gnette. She presumed I was the new curate. No loop-hole out of that. I had been seen at the theatre—not once nor twice. I could well believe it. The late Colonel Jameson, it appeared, had not approved of clergymen attending playhouses. She did not approve of it her-self. She presumed I realized the standing of this parish in the dio-cese? She dwelt on the force of example to the young. Of course, the opera—but that was widely different. She would suggest—she did suggest—not in the least vaguely. Sometime, perhaps, I would come to luncheon? She had really rather interested herself in the sermon yesterday—a little abrupt, possibly, at the close—still, of course, a young man, and not very experienced—besides, the Doctor had spoiled them for almost anybody else. Naturally.

The room widened after she had gone. You know these ladies with the thick atmosphere.

That night I went to the theatre. There's a stock company there for the summer and I have come to know one of the actors. He belongs to us—was married in the church last summer. The place was packed—always is—it's a good company. And Everett—he's the one—kept the house shouting. He's the regular funny man. The play that week was very funny anyhow—one of those things the billboards call a "scream." It was just that. Everett was the play. He stormed and galloped through his scenes until everybody was help-less. People like him; it's his third summer here. Well, at the end, nobody went. A lot of lads in the gallery began calling for Everett. We're common here; and not many of the quality patronize stock. Soon he pushed out from behind the curtain and made one of those fool speeches which generally fall flat. Only this one didn't.

Then I went "behind." The dressing rooms at the Alhambra are not home-like. Bare walls with a row of pegs along one side—a couple of chairs—a table piled with make-up stuff and over it a mirror flanked by electric lights with wire netting around them. Not gay. And grease paint, at close range, is not attractive. A man shouldn't cry after he's made up—that's a theatrical commandment, or ought to be. Probably a man shouldn't anyhow. But some do. I imagined Everett had, and that he'd done it with his head in his arms and his arms in the litter of the big table. I think I shook hands with him—one does inane things sometimes—but I don't know what I said. I had something like your experience—I just wasn't there for a minute or two.

Afterward, I went home with him—a long half-hour on the trol-ley, then up three flights into "light housekeeping" rooms in the back. There was cold meat on the table, and bread. The janitor's wife, good soul, had made a pot of coffee. "Light housekeeping" is a literal expression, let me tell you, and doctor's bills make it lighter. I followed him into the last room of the three. It looked different from the way I remembered it the afternoon before. When he turned the gas higher I saw why—the bed was gone—one of those stretcher things takes less room. Besides, they say it's better. So there she was—all that he had left of all that he had had—the girl he'd been mad about and married in our church a year ago. He wasn't even with her when she died; there was the Sunday afternoon rehearsal to attend. She wouldn't let him miss that. "Go on," she told him. "I'll wait for you." She didn't wait.

And he faced it down, he jammed it through, that young chap did—and was funny, oh, as funny as you can think, for hours, in front of hundreds of people. He never missed a cue, never bungled a line, and all the time seeing, up there in the light-housekeeping rooms, in the last room of them all, how she lay, in the utter silence.

Perhaps I shall come across a braver thing than that before I die, but I doubt it. I tried, of course, to get him not to do it. But it was very simple to him. It was his job. Nobody else knew the part; it was too late to substitute. The rest would lose their salaries if they closed down for the week, and God knew they needed them. So he said nothing—and was funny.

I don't know what you'd call it, but I think you know why I've told it to you. There's a splendor about it and a glory. To do one's job—isn't that the big thing, after all?

Meantime, mine's waiting for me on the other side of this desk. He has laid hands on every article in the room at least three times, and for the last few minutes has been groaning very loud. I think you'd like him—he's so alive.

Your letter saves me the cost of the western papers, and now that I know you'll—but you said not to write about you.

The Job has stopped groaning, and wants to know if I'm "writing all night just because, or, for the reason that."

It's night now—big night, and so still down-town here. Sometimes I stay up late to realize that I'm alive. The days are so crammed with happenings. And late at night seems so wide and everlasting. You've got the idea that I do things. Well, I don't. There are whole rows of days when it seems just a muddle of half-started attempts—a manner of hopeless confusion. There's a good deal of futility in it, first and last. That boy tonight for instance. And, sometimes, I get to wondering if, after all, one has the right to meddle in other people's lives. It's curious, but with you I've been quite sure. Always it has been as clear as light to me that you must come through this—that it will be right. I don't know how. Even that day you came, I was sure. As soon as *you* are sure, the thing is done. That man isn't to be worried about—or the doctors. Easy for me to say, isn't it?

Are you interested to know that I'm to have my building on the West Side? There was a meeting today. It's the best thing that's happened yet, that is, parochially. Maybe she's human after all. I mean Mrs. Jameson. She's going to pay for it.

I think that's all. You can't say I've tried to thunder at you this time. I really didn't last time. I've known all along that you wouldn't be impressed by thunder. The answer to that young devil's question seems to be: I'm writing "for the reason that," and not, "just because." Every time I think of that boy's name I have to laugh.

GEOFFREY McBIRNEY.

September 17th.

MY DEAR MR. McBIRNEY —

What *is* the boy's name? It must be queer if you laugh every time you think of it. Don't forget to tell me.

Your letters leave me breathless with things to say back. I suppose that's inspiration, to make people feel full of new ideas, and that you're crammed with it. In the first place I'm in a terrible hurry to tell you that something really big has touched the edge of my anaemic life, and that I have recognized it; I'm pleased that I recognized it. Listen — please — this is it. Robert Halarkenden; I must tell you who he is. Thirteen years ago my uncle was on a camping trip in Canada and one of the guides was a silent Scotchman, mixed in with French-Canadian habitants and half-breed Indians. My uncle was interested in him — he was picturesque and conspicuous — but he would not talk about himself. Another guide told Uncle Ted all that anyone has ever known about him, till yesterday. He was a guardian of the club and lived alone in a camp in the wildest part of it, and in summer he guided one or two parties, by special permission of the club secretary. This other guide had been to his cabin and told my uncle that it was full of books; the guide found the number astounding — "*effrayant.*" Also he had a garden of forest flowers, and he knew everything about every wild thing that grew in the woods. Well, Uncle Ted was so taken with the man that he asked the secretary about him, and the secretary shook his head. All that he could tell was that he was a remarkable woodsman and a perfect guide and that he had been recommended to him in the first place by Sir Archibald Graye of Toronto, who had refused to give reasons but asked as a personal favor that the man should be given any job he wished. This is getting rather a long story. Of course you know that the man was Halarkenden and you are now to know that my uncle brought him to Forest Gate as his gardener. He thought over it a day when Uncle Ted asked him and then said that he had lived fifteen years in the forest and that now he would like to live in a garden; he would come if Uncle Ted would let him make a garden as beautiful as he wished. Uncle Ted said yes, and he has done it. You have never seen such a garden—no one ever has. It is four acres and it lies on the bluff above the lake; that was a good beginning. If you had seen the rows of lilies last June, with pink roses blossoming through them, you would have known that Robert Halarkenden is a poet and no common man. Of course we have known it all along, but in thirteen years one gets to take miracles for granted. Yesterday I went down into the wild garden which lies between the woods and the flowers—this is a large place—and I got into the corner under the pines, and lay flat on the pink-brown needles, all warm with splashes of September sunlight, and looked at the goldenrod and purple asters swinging in the breeze and wondered if I could forget my blessed bones and live in the beauty and joy of just things, just the lovely world. Or whether it wouldn't be simpler to pull a trigger when I went back to my room, instead of kicking and struggling day after day to be and feel some other way. I get so sick and tired of fighting myself—you don't know. Anyhow, suddenly there was a rustle in the gold and purple hedge, and there was Robert Halarkenden. I wish I could make you see him as he stood there, in his blue working blouse, a pair of big clippers in his hand, his thick, half-gray, silvery thatch of hair bare and blowing around his scholar's forehead, his bony Scotch face solemn and quiet. His deep-set eyes were fixed with such a gentle gaze on me. We are good friends, Robin and I. I call him Robin; he taught me to when I was ten, so I always have. "You're no feeling well, lassie?" he asked; he has known me a long time, you see. And I suddenly sat up and told him about my old bones. I didn't mean to; I have told no one but you; not Uncle Ted even. But I did. And "Get up, lassie, and sit on the bench. I will talk to you," said Robin. So we both sat down on the rustic bench under the blowy pines, and I cried like a spring torrent, and Robin patted my hand steadily, which seems an odd thing for one's uncle's gardener to do, till I got through. Then I laughed and said, "Maybe I'll shoot myself." And he answered calmly, "I hope not, lassie." Then I said nothing and he said nothing for quite a bit, and then he began talking gently about how everybody who counted had to go through things. "A character has to be hammered into the likeness of God," he said. "A soul doesn't grow beautiful by sunlight and rich earth," and he looked out at his scarlet and blue and gold September garden and smiled a little. "We're no like the flowers." Then he considered again, and then he asked if it would interest me at all to hear a little tale, and I told him yes, of course. "Maybe it will seem companionable to know that other people have faced a bit of trouble," he said. And then he told me. I don't know if you will believe it; it seems too much of a drama to be credible to me, if I had not heard Robert Halarkenden tell it in his entirely simple way, sitting in his workingman's blouse, with the big clippers in his right hand. Thirty years before he had been laird of a small property in Scotland, and about to marry the girl whom he cared for. Then suddenly he found that she was in love with his cousin—with whom he had been brought up, and who was as dear as a brother—and his cousin with her. In almost no more words than I am using he told me of the crisis he lived through and how he had gone off on the mountains and made his decision. He could not marry the girl if she did not love him. His cousin was heir to his property; he decided to disappear and let them think he was dead, and so leave the two people whom he loved to be happy and prosperous without him. He did that. Two or three people had to know to arrange things, and Sir Archibald Graye, of Toronto, was one, but otherwise he simply dropped out of life and buried himself in Canadian forests, and then, just as he was growing hungry for some things he could not get in the forest, my uncle came along and offered him what he wanted.

"But how could you?" I asked him. "You're a gentleman; how could you make yourself a servant, and build a wall between yourself and nice people?"

Robin smiled at me in a shadowy, gentle way he has. "Those walls are a small matter of dust, lassie," he said. "A real man blows on them and they're tumbling. And service is what we're here for. And all people are nice people, you'll find." And when, still unresigned, I said more, he went on, very kindly, a little amused it seemed. "Why should it be more important for me to be happy than for those two? I hope they're happy," he spoke wistfully. "The lad was a genius, but a wild lad too," and he looked thoughtful. "Anyhow, it was for me to decide, you see, and a man couldn't decide ungenerously. That would be to tie one's self to a gnawing beast, which is what is like the memory of your own evil deed. Take my word for it, lassie, there was no other way."

"It seems all exaggerated," I threw at him; "there was no sense in your giving up your home and traditions and associations—it was unreasonable, fantastic! And to those two who had taken away your happiness anyhow."

I wish you could have heard how quietly and naturally Robert Halarkenden answered me. He considered a moment first, in his Scotch way, and then he said: "Do not you see, lassie, that's where it was simple, verra simple. Houses and lands and a place in the world are small affairs after love, and mine was come to shipwreck. So it seemed to me I'd try living free of the care of possessions. I'd try the old rule, that a man to find his life must lay it down. It was verra simple, as I'm telling you, once I'd got the fancy for it. Laying down a life is not such a hard business; it's only to make up your mind. And I did indeed find life in doing it, I was care-free as few are in those forest years."

I think you would have agreed with me, Mr. McBirney, that the middle-aged, lined face of my uncle's gardener was beautiful as he said those things. "Why did you leave the forest?" I asked him then; you may believe I'd forgotten about my bones by now.

"Ah, you'll find it grows irksome to be coddling one's own soul indefinitely," he confided to me with the pretty gentleness which breaks through his Scotch manner once in a while. "One gets tired of one's self, the spoiled body. I hungered to do something for somebody besides Robert Halarkenden. I'd taken charge of a lad with tuberculosis one summer up there, and I'd cured him, and I had a thought I could do the same for other lads. I wanted to get near a city to have that chance. I've been doing it here," and then he drew back into his Scotchness and was suddenly cold and reserved. But I knew that was shyness, and because he had spoken of his secret good deeds and was uncomfortable.

So I was not frozen. "You have!" I pounced on him. And I made him tell me how, besides his unending gardening, besides his limitless reading, he has been, all these years, working in the city in his few spare hours, spending himself and his wages—wages!—and helping, healing, giving all the time—like you— —

I felt the most torturing envy of my life as I listened to that. *I* wanted to be generous and wonderful and self-forgetting, and have a great, free heart "of spirit, fire, and dew." *I* wanted the something in me that made that still radiance of Robert Halarkenden's eyes. You see? "I"—always "I." That's the way I'm made. Utterly selfish. I can't even see heavenliness but I want to snatch it for myself. Robin never thought once that he was getting heavenliness—he only thought that he was giving help. Different from me. And all these years that I have been prancing around his garden of delight in two hundred dollar frocks—oh lots of them, for I'm rich and extravagant and I buy things because they're pretty and not because I need them—all these years he has been saving most of his seventy-five dollars a month, and getting sick children sent south, and never mentioning it. Why, I own a place south. I'm not such a beast but that—well, very likely I am a beast—I don't know. Anyhow, I've consistently lived the life of a selfish butterfly. And I cling to it. Despise me if you will. I do. I like my pretty clothes and my car, and how I do love my two saddle-horses! And I like dancing, too—I turn into a bird in the tree-tops when I dance, with not a care, not a responsibility. I don't want to give all that up. Have I got to? Have I *got* to "lay down my life" to find it? For, somehow, cling as I will to all these things, something is pushing, pushing back of them, stronger than them. You started it. I want the big things now—I want to be worth while. But yet clothes and gayety and horses and automobiles—I'm glued tight in that round. I don't believe I can tear loose. I don't believe I want to. Do you see—I'm in torment. And— silly idiot that I am—it's not for me to decide anything. I'm turning into a ton of stone—I'll be a horrible unhuman monster and have to give it all up and have nothing in return. Soon I'll lay down my life and *not* find it. I won't. I'll pull the trigger. Will I? Do you see how I vacillate and shiver and boil? This is my soul I'm pouring out to you. I hope you don't mind hot liquids. What you wrote about the actor made me sit still a whole half-hour without stirring a finger, with your letter in my hands. It was glorious—there's no question. You meant it to inspire me. But he had a job. I haven't. Back to me again, you see—unending me. Do you know about the man who used to say "Now let's go into the garden and talk about me"?

In any case, thank you for telling me that story. I'm glad to know that there are people like that—several of them. I know you and Robin anyhow, but the actor makes the world seem fuller of courage and worth-whileness. I wish a little of it would leak into—oh, *me* again. *Me* is getting "irksome," as Robin said. Remember to tell me the boy's name.

Yours gratefully if unsatisfactorily,
    AUGUST FIRST.

P. S.—Robert Halarkenden isn't his real name. It's his grandmother's father's name, and Welsh. I don't know the real one.

P. S. No. 2. If it isn't inconsistent, and if you think I'm worth while, you might pray just a scrap too. That I may get to be like you and Robin.

P. S. No. 3. But you know it's the truth that I'm balky at giving up everything in sight. I'd hate myself in bad clothes. *Can't* I have good ones and yet be worth while? Oh, I see. It doesn't matter if they're good or bad so long as I don't care too much. But I do care. Then they hamper me—eh? Is that the idea? This is the last postscript to this letter. Write a quick one—I'm needing it.

WARCHESTER,
    St. Andrew's Parish House,
        Sept. 23d.

I don't think it matters what his real name is. I'd been thinking all along, that he was just a convenient fiction, useful for an address, and now he turns out about the realest person going. Sometimes I imagine perhaps it will be like that when we get through with this world and wake up into what's after—that the things we've passed over pretty much here and been vague about will blaze out as the eternal verities. A miracle happened that day in your September garden. You've surely read *"Sur la Branche"*—that book written around a woman's belief in the Providence of God? Well, that's what I mean. Why did Halarkenden come down out of the woods into your uncle's garden? Why did you tell him, of all people? Why was it you who got through to the truth about him? Why did it all happen just the minute you most needed it? Of course I believe it — every word, exactly as you wrote it. It's impossible things like that which do happen and help us to bear the flatly ordinary. It's the incredible things that shout with reality. Miracles ought to be ordinary affairs — we don't believe in them because we're always straining every nerve to keep them from happening. We get so confused in the continual muddle of our own mistakes that when something does come straight through, as it was intended to do, we're like those men who heard the voice of God that day and told one another anxiously that it thundered.

Just think what went to make up those five minutes which gave you the lift you had to have — that young Scotchman, beating back his devils up in the lonely mountains all those years ago — that's when it started. And then fetch it down to now; his leaving home forever — and his exile in the woods — considerably different from a camping trip — the silent days, worse — the nights. And all the time his mind going back and back to what he'd left behind — his home, seeing every little corner of it — you know the tortures of imagination — his friends — the girl — always the girl — wondering why, and why, and why. Think of the days and months without seeing one of your own kind. He had to have books; his wild garden had to blossom. That man wasn't "coddling" his soul — he was ripping and tearing it into shreds and then pounding it together again with a hammer and with nails. All alone. That's the hardest, I suppose. And then, when it was all done and the worst of the pain and the torment passed, away up there in the forests, Robert Halarkenden — it *is* true, isn't it? — he rose from the dead, and being risen, he took a hand in the big business of the world. And his latest job is you. Has that occurred to you? I don't mean to say that he went through all that just to be a help to you. But I do say that if he hadn't gone through it he wouldn't have been a help to anybody. He did it. You needed to find out about it. He told you. It got through. Things sometimes do.

Suppose he hadn't come down from the mountains that day — that they'd found him there — that he hadn't had the nerve to face it? Who would have cured the tuberculosis lad — who would have sent the children south—who would have brushed through your uncle's garden hedge in Forest Gate, Illinois, and told you what you needed to be told? If *you* should turn out not to have the nerve—if, some day you—? Then what about *your* job? Nobody can ever do another person's real work, and, if it isn't done, I think it's likely we'll have to keep company with our undone, unattempted jobs forever. Mostly rather little jobs they are, too—so much the more shame for having dodged them. You say that you haven't got one. Maybe not, just now. But how do you know it isn't right around the corner? Did Halarkenden have you in mind those years he fought with beasts? No—not you—it was the girl back in Scotland. But here you are, getting the benefit of it. It's a small place, the world, and we're tied and tangled together—it won't do to cut loose. That spoils things, and it's all to come right at the last, if we'll only let it.

Possibly you'll think it's silly or childish, but I believe maybe this life with its queer tasks and happenings is just the great, typical Fairy Story, with Heaven at the last. They're true—that's why unspoiled children love fairy stories. They begin, they march with incident, best of all, one finds always at the end that "'They' lived happily ever afterward." "They," is you, and I hope it's me. The trouble with people mainly is that they're too grown up. Who knows what children see and hear in the summer twilights, on the way home from play? There's the big, round moon, tangled in the tree-tops—one remembers that—and there's the night wind, idling down the dusty street. Surely, though, more than that, but we've forgotten. Isn't growing up largely a process of forgetting, rather than of getting, knowledge? Of course there's cube-root and partial payments and fear and pain and love—one does acquire that sort of thing—but doesn't it maybe cost the losing of the right point of view? And that's too expensive. Naturally, or, perhaps, unnaturally, we can't afford to be caught sailing wash-tub boats across the troubled seas of orchard grass, or watching for fairies in the moonlight, but can't we somehow continue to want to give ourselves to similar adventure? There's a good deal of difference, first and last, between childishness and childlikeness—enough to make the one plain foolishness, and the other the qualification for entrance into the Kingdom of God. I'd rather have let cube-root go and have kept more of my imagination. The other day, in the middle of a catechism I was holding in the parish school, a small youngster rose to his feet and solemnly assured the company present that "the pickshers of God in the church" were "all wrong." Naturally we argued, which was a mistake. He got me. "God," said he, "is a Spirit, and spirits don't look like those colored pickshers in the windows." You see, he knew. He still remembers. But the higher mathematics and a few brisk sins will assist him to forget. Too bad. Still, when we get back home again surely it will all "come back" like a forgotten language.

Meantime there are two hundred dollar frocks to consider, as well as miracles in gardens. And that's all right, so long as the frocks are worthy the background, which I venture to suppose, of course, they are. The subject of clothes interests me a good deal just now, as I'm engaged in living on my salary. It's all a question of what one can afford, financially and spiritually. I gather you're not a bankrupt either way. I don't recall anything in Holy Writ that seems to re-quire dowdiness as necessary to salvation. If one's got money it's fortunate—if money's got one—that's different. Which is my plati-tudinous way of agreeing with the last postscript of your letter. I know you're getting to look at things properly again. To lose one's life certainly does not mean to kill it, and to give it away one needn't fling it to the dogs. And when you do connect with your job you'll recognize it and you'll know how to do it. I'd like to watch you. Once get your imagination going properly again and the days are rose and gold. Oh, not all of them—but a good many—enough.

I nearly forgot about Theodore. There's humor for you— Theodore, "The Gift of God"—that's the name they gave him sixteen good years ago somewhere over in Scotland as you'd have guessed from the rest of it, which is Alan McGregor. He is an orphan, is Theodore, but he doesn't wear the uniform of the Orphans' Home— far from it! He wears soft raiment and lives in kings' houses, or what amounts to the same thing. I am engaged in exorcising the devil out of him and in teaching him enough Latin to get into a decent school at the earliest instant. The Latin goes well—three nights a week from eight to half-past nine. But the devil takes ad-vantage of every one of those nine points of law which possession is said to give, and doesn't go at all. I am the only living person who knows how to define "charm." Charm is the most conspicuous at-tribute of the devil, and young McGregor has got it. Likewise other qualities, the ones, for instance, which make his name so rather awfully funny. You'd have to know Theodore to appreciate just how funny.

It was the rector who "wished" him on to me. The rector is one of his guardians, and being Theodore's guardian is a business which requires at least one undersecretary, and I'm that. Theodore and hot water have the strongest affinity known to psychological chemistry. So I'm kept busy. But it's all the keenest sport you can imagine, and it's going to be tremendously worth while if I can make a success of it. He's the right kind of bad, and he's getting ready to grow into a great, big, straight out-and-outer, with a mind like lightning and a heart like one of the sons of God. But that kind is always the worst risk. He has the weapons to get him through the fight with splendor, only they're every one two-edged, and you have to be careful with swords that cut both ways. His father was an inventor genius and there are bales of money and already it has begun to press down on him a little. Still, that may be the exact right thing. He has talked about it once or twice as a nice boy would. There's a place on the other side which comes to him, with factories and such things. He wanted to know wouldn't it be his business to see that the working people were properly looked after; I gathered he's been reading books, trying to find out. And then he got suddenly shy and very bright red as to the face, and cleared out. So far, so good, but it isn't far enough. Not yet.

That's my present job. You'll get yours.

Wasn't it wonderful—I mean Halarkenden! When I think of him and then of myself it gives me a good deal of a jounce. It surprises me that I ever had the conceit to think I could handle this parson proposition. Lately I've not been over-cheerful about it. That's one reason why your letter did me good.

I hear the Gift of God coming up the stairs, and I've neglected to look up the Future Periphrastic Conjugation and that ticklish difference between the Gerund and the Gerundive, which is vital.

One thing more—your second postscript. You didn't suppose that I don't, did you? Only, not like me!

GEOFFREY McBIRNEY.

The man took the letter down the three flights to the post-box at the entrance of the Parish House and dropped it, with a certain deliberation, as if he were speaking to someone whom he cared for, with a certain hesitation, as if he were not sure that he had spoken well, into the box. As he mounted the stairs again his springing gait was slower than usual. It was very late, but he drew a long chair close and poked the hard-coal fire till it glowed to him like a bed of jewels, all alive and stirred to their hot hearts; opals and topazes and rubies and cairngorms and the souls of blue sapphires and purple amethysts playing ghostly over the rest. He dropped into the chair and the tall, black-clothed figure fell into lax lines; his long fingers, the fingers of an artist, a musician, lay on the arms of the chair limply as if disconnected from any central power; there was surely despair, hopelessness, in the man's attitude. His gray eyes glowed from under the straight black brows with much of the hidden flame, the smouldering intensity of the coals at which he gazed. He sat so perhaps half an hour, staring moodily at the orange heart of the fire. Then suddenly, with a smothered half-syllable, with a hand thrown out impatiently, he was on his feet with a bound, and with that his arms were against the tall mantel and his head dropped in them, and he was gazing down so and talking aloud, rapidly, disjointedly, out of his loneliness, to his friend, the red fire. "How can I—how dare I? A square peg in a round hole—and the extra corners all weakness and wickedness. Selfishness—incompetence—I to set up to do the Lord's special work! I to preach to others—If it were not blasphemy it would be a joke—a ghastly joke. I can't go on—I have to pull out. Yet—how can I? They'll think—people will think—oh what *does* it matter what people will think? Only—if it hurt the rector—if it hurt the work? And Theodore—but—someone else would do him—more good than I can. There ought to be—an older man—to belong. Surely God will look after His gift—His gift!" The quick lightning of the brilliant eyes, which in this man often took the place of a smile, flashed; then the changing face was suddenly grim with a wrenching feeling, yet bright with a wind of tenderness not to be held back. The soul came out of hiding and wrote itself on the muscles of the face. "She—that's it—that's the gist of it—fool that I am. To think—to dream—to dare to hope. But I *don't* hope," he brought out savagely, and flung his shoulders straight and caught the wooden shelf with a grip. "I don't hope—I just"—the voice dropped, and his head fell on his arms again. "I won't say it. I'm not utterly mad yet." He picked up the poker and stirred the fire, and put on coal from a scuttle, and went and sat down again in the chair. "Something has got to be decided," he spoke again to the coals in the grate. "I've got to know if I ought to stay at this job, or if it's an impertinence." For minutes then he was silent, intent, it seemed, on the fire. Then again he spoke in the low, clear voice whose simplicity, whose purity reached, though he did not know it, the inmost hearts of the people to whom he preached. "I will make a test of her," he said, telling the fire his decision. "If she is safe and wins through to the real things, I'll believe that I've been let do that, and that I'm fit for work. If she doesn't—if I can't pull off that one job which is so distinctly put up to me—I'll leave." With a swing he had put out the lights in the big, bare living-room and gone into the bedroom beyond. He tried to sleep, but the tortured nerves, the nerves of a high-bred race-horse, eager, ever ready for action, would not be quiet. The great, rich city, the great poverty-stricken masses seething through it, the rushing, grinding work of the huge parish, had eaten into his youth and strength enormously already in six months. He had given himself right and left, suffered with the suffering, as no human being can and keep balance, till now he was, unknowingly, at the edge of a breakdown. And the distrust of his own fitness, the forgetfulness that, under one's own limitations, is an unlimited reserve which is the only hope of any of us in any real work; this was the form of the retort of his overwrought nerves. Yet at last he slept.

Meantime as he slept the hours crept away and it was morning and an early postman came and opened the box with a rattling key and took out three letters which the deaconess had sent to her scattered family, and one, oddly written, which the janitor had executed for his mother in Italy, and the letter to the girl. From hand to hand it sped, and away, and was hidden in a sack in a long mail-train, and at last, Robert Halarkenden, on the 25th of September, came down the garden path, and the girl, reading in the wild garden, laid aside her book and watched him as he came, and thought how familiar and pleasant a sight was the gaunt, tall figure, pausing on the gravelled walk to touch a blossom, to lift a fallen branch, as lovingly as a father would care for his children. "A letter, lassie," Robert Halarkenden said, and held out the thick envelope; and then did an extraordinary thing for Robert Halarkenden. He looked at the address in the unmistakable, big, black writing and looked at the girl and stood a moment, with a question in his eyes. The girl flushed. "Checkmate in six moves" was quite enough to say to this girl; one did not have to play the game brutally to a finish.

She laughed then. "I knew you must have wondered," she said, and with that she told the story of the letters.

"It's no wrong," Robert Halarkenden considered.

The girl jumped to her answer. "Wrong!" she cried, "I should say not. It's salvation—hope—life. Maybe all that; at the least it's the powers of good, fighting for me. Something of the sort—I don't know," she finished lamely. With that she was deep in her letter and Robert Halarkenden had moved a few yards and was tending a shrub that seemed to need nursing.

October the Sixth.

MY DEAR MR. McBIRNEY—

"The night wind idling down the dusty street"—You do make patterns out of the dictionary which please me. But I know that irritates you, for words are not what you are paying attention to—of course—if they were, yours wouldn't be so wonderful. It's the wind of the spirit that blows them into beautiful shapes for you, I suppose. To let that go, for it's immaterial—you think I might have a job? I? That I might do a real thing for anybody ever? If you only knew me. If you only could see the mountains of whipped cream and Maraschino cherries, the cliffs of French clothes and automobiles, the morasses of afternoon teas and dances and calls and luxury in general that lie between me and any usefulness. It's the maddest dream that I, with my bones and my money and my bringing up, all my crippling ailments, could ever, *ever* climb those mountains and cliffs and wade through those bogs. It's mad, I say, you visionary, you man on the other side of all that, who are living, who are doing things. I never can—I never can. And yet, it's so terrible, it's so horrible, so frightening, so desperate, sometimes, to be drowning in luxury. I woke in the night last night and before my eyes had opened I had flung out my hand and cried out loud in the dark: "What shall I do with my life—Oh what shall I do with my life?" And it isn't just me—though that's the burning, close question to my simple selfishness. But it's a lot of women—a lot. We're waking all over the world. We want to help, to be worth while; to help, to count. It won't do much longer to know French and Italian and play middling tennis and be on the Altar Society. You know what I mean. All that—yes—but beyond that the power which a real person carries into all that to make it big. The stronger you are the better your work is. I want to be strong, to be useful, to touch things with a personality which will move them, make them go, widen them. How? How can I? What can I do, ever? Oh what *can* I do— *what* can I do—with my life! I thought that day in August that it was only my illness, and my tie to an unloved man, but it's more than that. You have broadened the field of my longing, my restlessness, till it covers—everything. Help me then, for you have waked me to this want, question, agony. It's not only if I may kill my life—it's what I can do if I don't kill it. What can I do? Do you feel how that's a sharp, vital question to me? It's out of the deep I'm calling to you—do you know that? And it's my voice, but it's the voice of thousands—*now* you're in trouble. Now you wish you'd let me alone, for here we are at the woman question! I can see you shy at that. But I'm not going to pin you, for you only contracted to help me; I'll shake off the other thousands for the present. And, anyhow, can you help me? Oh, you have—you've delayed my—crime, I suppose it is. You've given me glimpses of vistas; you've set me reading books; widened every sort of horizon; you've even made me dream of a vague, possible work, for me. Yes, I've been dreaming that; a specific thing which I might do, even I, if I could cancel some house-parties, and a trip to France, and the hunting. But even if I could possibly give up those things, there's Uncle Ted. He's not well, and my dream would involve leaving him. And I'm all he has. We two are startlingly alone. After all, you see, it's a dream; I'm not big enough to do more than that—dream idly. Robin has a queer scheme just now. There's a bone-ologist here, the most famous one of the planet, exported from France, to cure the small son of one of the trillionaires with which this place reeks, and Robin insists that I see that bone-ologist about my bones. It's unpleasant, and I hate doctors and I don't know if I will. But Robin is very firm and insists on my telling Uncle Ted otherwise. I can't bother Uncle Ted. So I may do it. Yet, if the great man pronounced, as he would, that the other doctors were right, it would be almost going through the first hideous shock over again. So I may *not* do it. I must stop writing. I have a guest and must do a party for her. She's a California heiress—oh fabulously rich—much richer than I. With splendid bones. I gave her a dance last night and this morning she's off on my best hunter with my fiancé—save the mark! He admires her, and she certainly is a nice girl, and lovely to look at, with eyes like those young mediaeval, brainless Madonnas. I'm so glad to have someone else play with him—with Alec. I dread him so. I hate, I *hate* to let him—kiss me. There. If you were a real man I couldn't have exploded into that. You're only the spirit of a thunder-storm, you know; I'll never see you again on earth; I can say anything. I do say anything, don't I? I can say—I do say—that you have dragged me from the bottomless pit; that if any good comes of me it is your good—that you—being a shadow, a memory, an incident—are yet the central figure of this world to me. If I fall back into the pit, that is not your affair—mine, mine only. The light that shines around you for me is the only kindly light that may save me. But it may not. I may fall back. I have the toy in the drawer yet—covered with letters. Good-by—I am yours always,

AUGUST FIRST.

WARCHESTER,
St. Andrew's Parish House,
October 8th.

You'll never see me again? You'll see me in three days unless you stop me with a telegram.

I have a curious feeling that all this has happened before—my sitting here in front of the fire writing to you at one o'clock in the morning. They say it's one part of the brain working a shade ahead of the rest. I don't believe that. I do not believe my brain is working at all. It's spinning around. For days I've been living in the Fourth

Dimension—something like that. It changes the values to have a new universe whirl up around one. New heavens and a new earth—that's it. I have given up trying to analyze it. Even if I didn't want to tell you I couldn't help it. I'm beyond that now, and—helpless. I never dreamed of its being like this. I never thought much about it, except vaguely, as anybody does, and here it's come and snatched away the world.

I don't know how this is going to get itself said. But I can't stop it. That frightens me, rather; I've been used to ordering myself about or, at least, to feeling that I could. But that seems to be over. I don't pretend that I didn't foresee it, or rather that I didn't recognize it right at the beginning. What I did was to put off reckoning with it.

I see that I'm going to say things wrong. You have got to overlook that; I can't help it. I told you my brain wasn't working. For days I've been in a maze. Then your letter came, late this afternoon, and that settled it. Do you know what you said? Do you? You said: "If you were a real man, I wouldn't have exploded like this." A real man—what do you *think* I am? That's what I want to know. You'll find out I'm real enough before you and I are done. Do you suppose that I have been reading your letters all these weeks—those letters in which you said yourself you put your soul—as though they were stock quotations? Did you think you were a numbered "case," that I was keeping notes about you in that neat filing-cabinet down in the office? Well, it hasn't been exactly that way.

Do you remember that day you were here? How it rained—how dark it was? Why, I've never seen you, really. I'm always trying to imagine your face.

I've got to talk to you—some things can't be written. You won't stop me. Do you suppose you can? You've got to give me a chance to talk—that's only square. No, I don't mean all that. I don't quite know what I'm saying. I mean, you will let me come, won't you? I'll go away again after; you needn't be afraid. That's fair, isn't it?

You see, it's been strange from the start, and so quick. You, in the middle of the storm that day—the things you said—the fearful tangle you were in. And then the letters—the wonderful letters! And we thought we were keeping it all impersonal. You, with your blazing individuality—you, impersonal! I can't imagine your face, but you've stripped the masks and conventions off your soul for me—I've looked at that. I couldn't help it, could I? I couldn't stop. I can't now. I can't look at anything else. There isn't anything else—it fills my world—it's blotted out what used to be reality.

You're hundreds of miles away—what are you doing? Sitting, with your white dress a rosy blur in the lamplight, reading, thinking, afraid—frightened at the doctors—shrinking at the thought of that damned, pawing beast? We'll drop that last—this isn't the time for that—not yet. Miles away you are—and yet you're here—the real you that you've sent me in the letters. Always you are here. I listen to your voice—I've got that—your voice, singing through my days—here in the silence and the firelight, outside in the night under the stars, always, everywhere, I hear you—calling me.

You see, my head's gone. Don't think though, that I don't know the risk this is. But there isn't any other way. Those four weeks you didn't write, when I thought you had gone under—that was when I began to see how it was with me. Since then I've gone on, living on your letters, until now I can't imagine living without them—and more. And yet I know this may be the end. That's the risk. But I can't go on like that any more. It's everything now, or nothing. I want to know what you are going to do about it. What are you thinking—what must you think—what will you say to me when I see you in your still garden of miracles? I've got to know. If you meant it—you said I was the centre of your world—it can't be true that you meant that. I the centre of your great, clean, wind-swept world of hill-tops and of visions? I, who haven't got the decent strength to hold my tongue, and keep my hands. But you did say that—you did! When I come, will you say it to me again, out loud, that? I can't imagine it—such a thing couldn't happen to me. But if you shouldn't—if you should tell me not to come—no, I can't face that. Where is the solution? I see perfectly that you can't care—why should you?—I see also that you must be made to. That's just it. I know what I must have and that I can never have it. No, that isn't so. I know that I shall come and take you away from what you fear and hate, out of the world we both know is not real, into reality. I shall tell you why I want you, why you must come. You will listen and you will answer. You will say why it's madness and insanity. I shall have to hear all your obvious reasons, but I shall know that you know they are lies—Do you think—do you dream, that they can stand between me and you? You can't stop me. Because I have seen your soul—you said so—you've held it out, in your two hands, for me to look at. You can't keep me away from you. I know how you'll fight against it. You won't win—don't count on it.

This isn't insolence—it's the thing that's got me. I can't help it. A man is that way. I don't half know what I've said; I don't dare read it. You have got to make it out yourself, somehow.

You've asked me questions. You're troubled, frightened—I know, it's—hell. Do you think I can sit here any longer and let you go through that alone? I've been over the whole thing—I've done nothing else, and out of the maze of it all I'm forced to come to this. It's the old way and the only one—the answer to it all. What can you do with your life—your life that is going to be, that is now, all glorious with loveliness and light? Give it away—that's it—give it to me, and then we two will set it to music and send it singing through the world. The old way. You to come home to when the day is done— your face, your hands, your eyes— —

You'll have to overlook this. It's mad to go on. It's mad anyway. If you knew how I've lied to myself, how I've struggled and fought and twisted to keep this back from you! And here it is, confused and grotesque and contradictory and wrong. If I could look at you and say it, I could get it right. If I could look at you—if I could see you. Give me a chance. Then I'll go away again—if you say so. I had to give you warning—it didn't seem square not. And I've bungled it like this! I tell you I can't help it. It's what you've done to me. I tried to spare you this, but I waited too long—now it's almighty.

Give me my man's chance—Oh I know I'm not worth it—who is? Afterwards—

G. McB.

October 10th.

Telegram received by the Reverend Geoffrey McBirney, St. Andrews Parish House, Warchester:

You must not come. Leaving Forest Gate. Sailing for Germany Saturday. Letter.

AUGUST FIRST.

The son of the under-gardener was a steady ten-year-old three hundred and sixty-four days of the year, and his Scottish blood commended him to Robert Halarkenden and inspired a confidence not justified on the three hundred and sixty-fifth day.

"Angus," said Halarkenden, regarding the boy with a blue glance like a blow, "the young mistress wishes this letter posted to catch the noon train. The master has sent for me and I canna take it. You will"—the bony hand fished in the deep pocket and brought out a nickel—"you will hurry with this letter and post it immediately." "Yes, sir," said Angus, and Robert Halarkenden turned to go to the master of the great house, ill in his great room, with no doubt about the United States mails. While Angus, being in the power of the three hundred and sixty-fifth day, trotted demurely into the meshes of Fate.

Fate was posing as another lad, a lad of charm and adventure. "C'm on, Ang," proposed Fate in nasal American; "Evans's chauffeur's havin' a rooster-fight in the garage. Hurry up—c'm on—lots of fun." And while Angus, stirred by the prospect, struggled with a Scotch conscience, the footman from next door sauntered up, a good-natured youth, and, stopping, caught the question.

"Get along to your chicken-fight," he adjured Angus, and took the letter from his hand. "I'm on my way to the post-office now. I'll mail it as good as you, ain't it?" And Angus fled up the street along with Fate. While Tom Mullins thrust the letter casually into a coat-pocket and dropped in to see his best girl, and, in a bit of horse-play with that lady, lost the letter. "Sure, I mailed it," he answered Angus's inquiries that afternoon, and Angus passed along the assurance, not going into details, and every one concerned was satisfied.

While, in a Parish House many miles down the railed roads that measure the country, a man waited. And waited, ever with a sicker restlessness, a more unendurable longing. Saturday came, and the man hoped, till the hour for any boat's sailing was long past, for a letter, another telegram. Then, "She has had it mailed after she left," he reasoned, and all of Monday and Tuesday he waited and watched and invented reasons why it might come to-morrow or even later—even from the other side—from Germany. Two weeks, three, and then four, he held to varying fictions about the letter, which Arline Baker, the lady of Tom Mullins's heart, had picked up from the floor that day in October and tucked into a bureau drawer to give to Tom—tucked under a summer blouse. And the weather had turned chilly, helping along Fate as weather will at times, and the summer blouse had not been worn, and the letter had been forgotten.

Then there came a day when he took measures with himself, because suspense and misery were eating his strength. He faced the situation; he had poured his heart, keeping back nothing, at her feet. And she had not answered, except with a few words of a telegram. He knew, by that, that she had got his letter, the first love-letter of his life. But she had not cared enough to answer it. Or else, his faith in her argued, something had happened, there had been some unimaginable reason to prevent her answering. That the letter had been lost was so commonplace a solution that it did not occur to him. One does not think of mice setting off gunpowder magazines. At all events he was facing a stone wall; there was no further step to take; she must be in Germany; he did not know her address; if he did, how could he write again? A man may not hound a woman with his love. Yet he was all but mad with anxiety about her, beyond this other suffering. Why had she suddenly gone to Germany? What did that mean? In his black struggles for enlightenment, he believed sometimes that, in a fantastic attack of *noblesse oblige*, she had married the other man and gone to Germany with him. That thought drove him near insanity. So he gathered up, alone before his fire, all these imaginings and doubts, and sat with them into the night, and made a packet of them, and locked them away, as well as he might, into a chamber of his memory. And the next day he flung himself into his work as he had not been able ever to do before; he made it his world, and resolutely shut out the buoyant voice and the personality so intimately known, so unknown. He tried to be so tired, at night, that he could not think of her; and he succeeded far enough to make living a possibility, which is all that any of us can do sometimes. Often the thought of her, of her words, of her letters, of the gay voice telling of a hideous future, stabbed him suddenly in the night, in the crowded day. But he put it aside with a mighty effort each time, and each time gained control.

And then it was May, and in June he was to have his vacation. And once more the doubt of his fitness for his work was upon him. The stress of the tremendous gait of the big parish, and the way he had thrown his strength by handfuls into the work, had told. If a healthy and happy man uses brain and heart and body carefully it is perhaps true that he cannot overwork. But if a high-strung man gives himself out all day long, every day, recklessly, and is at the same time under a mental strain, he is likely to be ill. Geoffrey McBirney was close to an illness; his attitude toward life was warped; he was reasoning that he had made the girl a test case and that the case had failed; that it was now his duty to stand by the test and give up his work. And then, one day, the letter came. The weather had turned warm in Forest Gate and Arline Baker had got out her summer blouses.

October 10th [it was dated].

This morning, after I had read your letter it was as if I were being beaten to earth by alternate blows, like thunder, like lightning, fierce and beautiful and terrible, of joy and of grief.

For I care—I care—I can't wait to tell you—I'm so glad, so triumphant, so wretched that I care—that it's in me to care, desperately, as much as any woman or man since the foundation of the world. It's in me—once you said it wasn't—and you have brought it to life, and I care—I love you. I want to let you come so that it left me blind and shaking to send that telegram. But there isn't any question. If I let you come I would be wicked. I, with my handful of broken life, to let you manacle your splendid years to a lump of stone? Could you think I would do that? Don't you see that, because I care, I'm so much more eager not to let you? I'm selfish and my first answer to that letter was a rush of happiness. I forgot there was anything in time or space except the flood which carried me out on a sea of just you—the sweeping, overwhelming many waters of—you. I wonder if you'd think me brazen if I told you how it seemed? As if your arms were around me, and the world reeling. Some of those clever psychologists, James or Lodge, I can't remember who, have a theory that to higher beings the past and present and future are all one; no divisions in eternity. It seemed like that. Questions and life and right and wrong all dissolved in the white heat of one fact. I didn't see or hear or know. I put my head on the table, on your writing, in my locked room, and simply felt—your arms.

If this were to be a happy love-affair I couldn't write this; I would have decent reserve—I hope; I would wait, maybe, and let you find out things slowly. But there isn't time—oh, there isn't any time. I have to tell you now because this is the last. You can't write again; I won't let you throw away your life; I'm not worth much, generally speaking, but I'm worth your salvation just now if I have the strength to give it to you. And I'm staggering under the effort, but I'm going to give it to you. I'm going to keep you away.

It was realizing that I must do this which beat me to earth with those terrible, bright, sharp swords. You see I'm starting off suddenly with Uncle Ted. He is very ill, with heart trouble, and the doctors think his chance is to get to Nauheim at once. It was decided last night, and we had passage engaged for Saturday within an hour, and then this morning the letter came. As soon as I could pull myself together a little I began to see how things were, and it looked to me as if somebody—God maybe—had put down a specific hand to punish my useless life and arrange your salvation. My going away is the means He is using.

For you are such a headstrong unknown quantity, that if I had seen you, I couldn't have held you, and how could I have fought the exquisite sweetness and glamour that is through even your written words, that would make me wax in your hands, if you had been here and I had heard your voice and seen your eyes and felt your touch; oh, I would have done it—I *must* do it—but it would have killed me I think. It's more possible this way.

For I'm going indefinitely and all I have to do is to suppress my address. Just that. You can't find it out, for Robin is going away too; he is to do some work of mine while I am gone; and you can't come here and inquire for "August First," can you, now? So this is all—the end. Suddenly I feel inadequate and leaden. It is all over—the one chance for real happiness which I have had in my butterfly days—over. But you have changed earth and heaven—I want you to know it. I can't even now say that if Uncle Ted shouldn't need me; if the hideous, creeping monster should begin its work visibly on me, that I might not some day use the pistol. But I do say that because of you I will try to make any living that I may do count for something, for somebody. I am trying. You are to know about that in time.

And now the color is going out of my life—you are going. Some day you will care for some one else more than you think now you care for me. I'm leaving you free for that—but it's all I can do. Why must my life be wreck and suffering? Why may I not have the common happinesses? Why may I not love you—be there for you "at the end of the day"? The blows are raining hard; I'm beaten close to earth. Has God forsaken me? I can only cling tight to the thin line of my duty to Uncle Ted; I can't see any further than that. Good-by.

AUGUST FIRST.

The man shook as if in an ague. He laid the letter on a table and fastened it open with weights so that the May breeze, frolicking through the top of the Parish House, might not blow it away. Standing over it, bending to it, sitting down, he read it and re-read it, and paced the room and came back and bent over it. He groaned as he looked at the date. Seven months ago if he had had it—what could have held him? She loved him—what on earth could have kept him from her, knowing that? Not illness nor oceans or her will. No, not her will, if she cared; and she had said it. He would have swept down her will like a tidal wave, knowing that.

Seven months ago! He would have followed her to Germany. He laughed at the thought that she believed herself hidden from him. The world was not big enough to hide her. What was a trip to Germany—to Madagascar? But now—where might she not be—what might not have happened? She might be dead. Worse—and this thought stopped his pulse—she might be married.

That was the big, underlying terror of his mind. In his restless pacing he stopped suddenly as if frozen. His brain was working this way and that, searching for light. In a moment he knew what he would do. He dashed down the familiar steep stairs; in four minutes more he had raced across the street to the rectory, and brought up, breathless, in the rector's study.

"What's the matter—a train to catch?" the rector demanded, regarding him.

"Just that, doctor. Could I be spared for three days?"

The rector had not failed to have his theories about this brilliant, hard-working, unaccountable, highly useful subaltern of his. His heart had one of its warmest spots for McBirney. Something was wrong with him, it had been evident for months; one must help him in the dark if better could not be done.

"Surely," said the rector.

There was a fast train west in an hour; the man and his bag were on it, and twenty-four hours later he was stumbling off a car at the solid, vine-covered, red brick station at Forest Gate. An inquiry or two, and then he had crossed the wide, short street, the single business street of the rich suburb, facing the railway and the station, and was in the post-office. He asked about one Robert Halarkenden. The postmaster regarded him suspiciously. His affair was to sort letters, not to answer questions. He did the first badly; he did not mean to do the other at all.

"No such person ever been in town," he answered coldly, after a moment's staring. The man who had hurried a thousand miles to ask the question, set his bag on the floor and faced the postmaster grimly.

"He must have been," he stated. "I sent a lot of letters to him last year, and they reached him."

"Oh—last year," the official answered stonily. "He might 'a' been here last year. I only came January." And he turned with insulted gloom to his labors.

McBirney leaned as far as he might into the little window. "Look here," he adjured the man inside, "do be a Christian about this. I've come from the East, a thousand miles, to find Halarkenden, and I know he was here seven months ago. It's awfully important. Won't you treat me like a white man and help me a little?"

Few people ever resisted Geoffrey McBirney when he pleaded with them. The stolid potentate turned back wondering, and did not know that what he felt stirring the dried veins within him was charm. "Why, sure," he answered slowly, astonished at his own words, "I'll help you if I can. Glad t' help anybody."

There was a cock-sure assistant in the back of the dirty sanctum, and to him the friend of mankind applied.

"Halarkenden—Robert," the assistant snapped out. "'Course. I remember. Gardener up to the Edward Reidses," and McBirney thrilled as if an event had happened. "Uncle Ted" was "the Edward Reidses." It might be her name—Reid.

"He went away six or seven months ago, I think," McBirney suggested, breathing a bit fast. "I thought he might be back by now."

"Nawp," said the cock-sure one. "I remember. 'Course. Family broke Up. Old man died."

"No, he didn't," the parson interrupted tartly. "He went to Germany."

"Aw well, then, 'f you know mor'n I do, maybe he did go to Germany. Anyhow, the girl got married. And Halarkenden, he ain't been around since. Leastaways, ain't had no letters for him." There was an undue silence, it appeared to the officials inside the window. "That all?" demanded Cocksure, thirsting to get back to work.

"What 'girl' do you speak of—who was married?" McBirney asked slowly.

"Old man's niece. Miss——"

But the name never got out. McBirney cut across the nasal speech. He would not learn that name in this way. "That's all," he said quickly. "Thank you. Good-by."

So Geoffrey McBirney went back to St. Andrews. And the last state of him was worse than the first.

WARCHESTER,
St. Andrew's Parish House,
May 26th.

RICHARD MARSTON, ESQ.
  C/r Marston & Brooks, Consulting Engineers,
   Boston.

DEAR DICK—

Of course I'll go, unless something happens, as per usual. I've got the last three weeks of June, and nowhere in particular to waste them at. Shall I come to Boston, or where do we meet? Let me know when we're to start; likewise what I am to bring. Do you take a trunk, or do we send the things ahead by express? I've never been on a long motor trip before. I'm mighty glad to go; it's just what I would have wanted to do, if I'd wanted to do anything. Doesn't sound eager, does it? What I mean is, it will be out-of-doors and I need that a good deal; and it will be with you, which I need more.

The chances are you won't find me gay. It's been a rotten winter, mostly, and it's left me not up to much. Not up to anything, in fact. Things have happened, and the bottom dropped out last autumn.

The fact is, I'm going to clear out. Try something else. I want to talk to you about that—I mean about the new job. I'd thought, maybe, of a school up in the country. I like youngsters. You remember that Scotch lad—the one with the money? I wrote you—I tutored him in Latin. That's where I got the notion. I had luck with him, And I've missed him a lot since. So maybe that's the thing. I don't know. We'll talk. Anyhow, this is ended.

I never let out what I thought about your being so decent, that night at college, when I said I was going to be a parson; the chances are I never will. But that's largely why I'm telling you this. I'm flunking my job—I have flunked it; the letter to the rector is written—he's to get it at the end of his holiday. I think I've stopped caring what other people will say, but I hate to hurt him. But you see, I thought it through, and it's the only thing to do—just to get out. I picked one definite job, for a sort of test, and it fell through. That settled it.

I wanted to tell you for old sake's sake. Besides, I somehow needed to have you know. And so now I'm going motoring with you. Write me about the trunk, and about when and where.

As ever,
MAC.

P. S. We needn't see people, need we?

The automobile with the two young men in the front seat sped smoothly over June roads. For a week they had been covering ground day after day; to-night they were due at Dick Marston's cousin's country house to stop for three days before the return trip through the mountains.

"Dick," reflected Geoffrey McBirney aloud, "consider again about dropping me in Boston. I'll be as much good at a house-party as a crape veil at a dance. You're an awful ass to take me."

"That's up to me," remarked Dick. "Get your feet out of the gears, will you? The Emorys are keen for you and I said I'd bring you, and I will if I have to do it by the scruff of the neck. Don Emory is away but will be back to-morrow."

"Splendid!" said McBirney, and then, "I won't kick and scream, you know. I'll merely whine and sulk," he went on consideringly. "I'll hate it, and I'll be ugly-tempered, and they'll detest me. Up to you, however."

"It is," responded Marston, and no more was said. So that at twilight they were speeding down the long, empty ocean drive with good salt air in their faces, and lights of cottages spotting the opal night with orange blurs. It was a large, gay house-party, and the person who had been called, it was told from one to another, "the young Phillips Brooks," a person who brought among them certain piquant qualities, was a lion ready to their hand. With the general friendliness of a good man of the world, there was something beyond; there was reality in the friendliness, yet impersonality — a detached attitude; the man had no axes to grind for himself; one felt at every turn that this important universe of the *haute monde* was unimportant to him. Through his civility there was an outcropping of savage honesty which made the house-party sit up straight, more than once. Emerson says, in a better-made sentence, that the world is at the feet of him who does not want it. Geoffrey McBirney had taken a long jump, years back, and cleared the childishness, lifelong in most of us, of wanting the world. There is an attraction in a person who has done this and yet has kept a love of humanity. Witness St. Francis of Assisi and other notables of his ilk.

The people at Sea-Acres felt the attraction and tried to lionize the dark, tall parson with the glowing, indifferent eyes. But the lion would not roar and gambol; the lion was a reserved beast, it seemed, with a suggestion of unbelievable, yet genuine, distaste under attentions. That point was alluring. One tried harder to soften a brute so worth while, so difficult. Three or four girls tried. The lion was outwardly a gentle lion, pleasant when cornered, but seldom cornered. He managed to get off on a long walk alone when Angela, of nineteen, meant him to have played tennis, on the second day.

The June afternoon was softening to a rosy dimness as he came in, very tired physically, hot and grimy, and sick of soul. "Glory be, tea-time's over, and they'll be dressing for dinner," he murmured, and turned a corner on eight of "them." A glance at the gay group showed two or three new faces. More guests! McBirney set his teeth. But he had no space to take note of the arrivals, for Angela spoke.

"Just in time, Mr. McBirney," Angela greeted him. "Don Emory's coming—see!" A car was spinning up the drive.

"Is he?" he answered perfunctorily. And the two words were clipped from history even as they were spoken, by a cry that rang from the group of people. Tod Winthrop ought to have been in bed. It was six-thirty, and he was four years old, but his mother had forgotten him, and his nurse had a weakness for the Emorys' second man; it was also certain that if a storm-centre could be found, he would be its nucleus. Out he tumbled from the shrubbery, exactly in front of the incoming automobile, as unpleasant a spoiled infant as could be imagined, yet a human being with a life to save. McBirney, standing in the drive, whirled, saw the small figure, ten feet down the drive, the machine close upon it; there was time for a man to spring aside; there was no time to rescue a child. A lightning wave of repulsion flooded him. "Have I got to throw myself down there and get maimed—for a fool child whom everybody detests?" Without words the thought flooded him, and then in a strong defiance, the utter honesty of his soul caught him. "I won't! I won't!" he shouted, and was conscious of the clamor of many voices, of a rush-ing movement, of a man's scream across the tumult: "It's too late—for God's sake *don't!*"

It was a day later when he opened his eyes. Dick Marston sat there.

"Shut up," ordered Dick.

"I haven't— —"

"No, and you won't—you're not to talk. Shut up. That's what you're to do."

The eyes closed; he was inadequate to argument. In five minutes they opened again.

"None of your eloquence now," warned Dick.

"One thing— —"

"No," firmly.

"But, Dick, it's torturing me. Was the child killed?"

Dick Marston's face looked curious. "Great Scott! don't you know what you— —"

McBirney groaned inwardly. "Yes, I know. I was a coward. But I've got to know if—the kid—was killed."

"Coward!" gasped Dick—and Geoffrey put out his shaking hand.

"In mercy, Dick"—he was catching his breath, flushing, laboring with each word—"don't—talk about—Was the boy—killed?"

"Killed, no, sound as a nut—but you— —"

"That's all," said McBirney, and his eyes closed, and he turned his face to the wall. But he did not go to sleep. He was trying to meet life with self-respect gone. The last thing he remembered was that second of utter rebellion against wrecking his strength, his good muscles—he had not thought of his life—to save the child. There had been no time to choose; his past, his character, had chosen for him, and they had branded him as that impossible thing, a coward. He put up his hand and felt bandages on his head; he must have got a whack after all in saving his precious skin. He remembered now. "Didn't jump quick enough, I suppose," he thought, with a sneer at the man in whose body he lived, the man who was himself, the man who was a coward. After a while he heard Dick Marston stir. He was bending over him.

"Got to go to dinner, old man," Dick said. "I wish you'd let me tell you what they all think about you."

McBirney shook his head impatiently, and Dick sighed heavily, and then in a moment the door shut softly.

Things were vague to him for hours longer, and a sleeping powder kept the next morning drowsy, but in the afternoon, when Marston came for his hourly look at the patient, "Dick," said the patient, "I want to talk to you."

"All right, old man," Dick answered, "but first just a word. I hate to bother you, but somebody's after you on long-distance. The fellow has telephoned three times — I was here the last time. He says — —"

The man with the bandages on his head groaned. "Don't," he begged and tossed his hand out. "I know what he's wanting. I can't talk to him. I don't want to hear. It's no use. Shut him off, Dick, can't you?"

"Sure, old man," Marston agreed soothingly. "Only, he says — —"

"Oh, don't — I know what it is — don't let him say it," pleaded the invalid, quite unreasonable, entirely obstinate.

A committee from the vestry of a city church had, unknown to him at the moment, come to Warchester to hear him preach the Sunday before he had left on his trip. A letter from the rector since had warned him that they were full of enthusiasm about his sermon and himself and that a call to the rectorship of the church was imminent. This was a preliminary of the call; there was no doubt in his mind about that. And knowing as he did how he was going to give up his work, writhing as he was under the last proof, as he felt it, of his unfitness, the thought of facing suave vestrymen even over a telephone, was a horror not to be borne.

"Tell 'em I'm dead, Dick, there's a good boy. I *won't* talk to anybody — to-day or to-morrow, anyhow."

"All right," Dick agreed. The patient was flushed and excited—it would not do to go on. "But the chap said he might run down here," he added, thinking aloud.

The patient started up on his elbow and glared. "Great Scott—don't let him do that; you won't let him get at me, Dick? I'm sorry to be such a poor fool, but—just now—to-day—two or three days—Dick, I *can't*"—he stammered out, his hands shaking, his face twisting. And Dick Marston, as gently as a woman might, took in charge this friend whom he loved.

"Don't you worry, Geoffie; the bears shan't eat you this trip. I'll settle the chap next time he calls up."

And McBirney fell back, with closed eyelids, relieved, secure in Dick's strength. He lay, breathing quickly, a moment or two, and then opened his eyes.

"When can I get away, Dick?"

"We'll start to-morrow if you're strong enough."

"You needn't go, Dicky. I'll get a train. I'm— —"

"None of that," said Marston. "Whither thou goest, for the present, I'll trot. But—Hope Stuart's anxious to—meet you."

"Who's Hope Stuart?"

Dick Marston hesitated, looked embarrassed. "Why—just a girl," he said. "But an uncommon sort of girl. She's done some—big things. Cousin of Don Emory's, you know. Came yesterday—just before your party. She—she's—well, she's different from the ruck of 'em—and she—said she'd like to meet you. I half promised she could."

McBirney flushed. "I *can't* see people, Dick," he threw back nervously. "They're kind—it's decent of them. I suppose, as long as the boy wasn't killed—" he stopped.

"Geoff, you've got some bizarre idea in your head about this episode, and I can't fathom it," spoke Dick Marston. "What do you think happened anyway?" he demanded. And stopped, horrified at the look on the other's face.

"Dick, you mean to be kind, but you're being cruel—as death," whispered Geoffrey McBirney. "I simply—can't bear any conversation—about that. I've got to cut loose and get off somewhere and—and—arrange."

His voice broke. Dick Marston's big hand was on his. "Old man," Dick said, "you're all wrong, but if you won't let me talk about it I won't—now. Look here—we'll sneak to-morrow. Everybody's going off in cars for an all-day drive, and I'll start, and pull out half-way on some excuse, and come back here, and you'll be packed, and we'll get out. I'll square it with Nanny Emory. She'll understand. I'll tell her you're crazy in the head, and won't be hero-worshipped."

"Hero-worshipped!" McBirney laughed bitterly to himself when Dick was gone. These good people, because he was a parson, because the child's blood, by some accident, was not on his head, were banded to keep his self-respect for him, to cover over his cowardice with some distorted theory of courage. Perhaps they did not know, but he knew, about that last thought of determined egotism, that shout of "I won't! I won't!" before the car caught him. He knew, and never as long as he lived could he look the world in the eyes again, with that shame in his soul. What would *she* have thought, had she been there to see? She would not have been deceived; her clear eyes would have seen the truth.

So he felt; so he went over and over the five minutes of the accident till all covering seemed to be stripped from his strained nerves.

"You'd better dress now and go down in the garden and sit there," suggested Dick the next morning. "Take a book, and wait for me there. The place will be empty in twenty minutes. I'll be along before lunch."

The garden rioted with color. The listless black figure strayed through the sunshine down a walk between a mass of scarlet Oriental poppies on one side and a border of swaying white lilies on the other.

Ranks of tall larkspur lifted blue spires beyond. The air was heavy with sweet smells, mignonette and alyssum and the fragrance of a thousand of roses, white and pink and red, over by the hedge.

The hedge ran on four sides of the garden, giving a comforting sense of privacy. In spite of the suffering he had gone through, the raw nerves of the man felt a healing pressure settling over them, resting on them, out of the scented stillness. There were no voices from the house; bees were humming somewhere near the rose-bushes; the first cricket of summer sang his sudden, drowsy song and was as suddenly quiet.

The black figure strayed on, down the long walk between the flowers, to a rustic summer-house, deep in vines, at the end of the path. There were seats there, and a table. He sat down in the coolness and stared out at the bright garden. He tried manfully to pull himself together; he reminded himself that he could still work, could still serve the world, and that, after all, was what he was in the world for. There was a reason for living, then; there was hope, he reasoned. And then, the hopelessness, the helplessness of under-vitality, which is often the real name for despair, had caught him again. His arms were thrown out on the rough table and his head lay on them.

There was a sound in the vine-darkened little summer-house. McBirney lifted his head sharply; a girl stood there, a slim figure in black clothes. McBirney sprang to his feet astonished, angry. Then the girl put out her hand and held to the upright of the opening as if to hold herself steady, and began talking in a hurried tone, as if she were reciting.

"I had to come to tell you that you were not a coward, but a hero, and that you saved Toddy Winthrop's life, and it's so, and Dick Marston says you don't know it and won't let him tell you and I've got to have you know it, and it's so and you have to believe it, for it's so." The girl was gasping, clutching the side of the summer-house with her face turned away, frightened yet determined.

"Who are you?" demanded McBirney, sternly, staring at her. There was something surging up inside of him, unknown, unreasonable; heart's blood was rushing about his system inconveniently; his pulse was hammering—why? He knew why; this sudden vision of a girl reminded him—took him back—he cut through that idea swiftly; he was ill, unbalanced, obsessed with one memory, but he would not allow himself to go mad.

"Who are you?" he repeated sternly. And the girl turned and faced him and looked up into his grim, tortured face, half shy, half laughing, all glad.

She spoke softly. "Hope," she said. "You needed me"—she said, "and I came."

With that, with the unreasonable certainty that happens at times in affairs which go beyond reason, he was certain. Yet he did not dare to be certain.

"Who are you?" he threw at her for the third time, and his eyes flamed down into the changing face, the face which he had never known, which he seemed to have known since time began. The laughter left it then and she gazed at him with a look which he had not seen in a woman's eyes before. "I think you know," she said. "Toddy Winthrop isn't the only one. You saved me—Oh, you've saved me too." Every inflection of the voice brought certainty to him; the buoyant, soft voice which he remembered. "I am Hope Stuart," she said. "I am August First."

"Ah!" He caught her hands, but she drew them away. "Not yet," she said, and the promise in the denial thrilled him. "You've got to know—things."

"Don't think, don't dream that I'll let you go, if you still care," he threw at her hotly. And with that the thought of two days before stabbed into him. "Ah!" he cried, and stood before his happiness miserably.

"What?" asked the girl.

"I'm not fit to speak to you. I'm disgraced; I'm a coward; you don't know, but I let—that child be killed as much as if he had not been saved by a miracle. It wasn't my fault he was saved. I didn't mean to save him. I meant to save myself," he went on with savage accusation.

"Tell me," commanded the girl, and he told her.

"It's what I thought," she answered him then. "I told the doctor what Dick said, this morning. The doctor said it was the commonest thing in the world, after a blow on the head, to forget the last minutes before. You'll never remember them. You did save him.

Your past—your character decided for you"—here was his own bitter thought turned to heavenly sweetness!—"You did the brave thing whether you would or not. You've got to take my word—all of our words—that you were a hero. Just that. You jumped straight down and threw Toddy into the bushes and then fell, and the chauffeur couldn't turn fast enough and he hit you—and your head was hurt."

She spoke, and looked into his eyes.

"Is that the truth?" he shot at her. It was vital to know where he stood, whether with decent men or with cowards.

"So help me God," the girl said quietly.

As when a gate is opened into a lock the water begins to pour in with a steady rush and covers the slimy walls and ugly fissures, so peace poured into the discolored emptiness of his mind. Suddenly the gate was shut again. What difference did anything make—anything?

"You are married," he stated miserably, and stood before her. The moments had rushed upon his strained consciousness so overladen, the joy of seeing her had been so intense, that there had been no place for another thought. He had forgotten. The thought which meant the failure of happiness had been crowded out. "You are married," he repeated, and the old grayness shadowed again a universe without hope.

And then the girl whose name was Hope smiled up at him through a rainbow, for there were tears in her eyes. "No," she answered, "no." And with that he caught her in his arms: her smile, her slim shoulders, her head, they were all there, close, crushed against him. The bees hummed over the roses in the sunshiny garden; the locust sang his staccato song and stopped suddenly; petals of a rose floated against the black dress; but the two figures did not appear to breathe. Time and space, as the girl had said once, were fused. Then she stirred, pushed away his arms, and stood erect and looked at him with a flushed, radiant face.

"Do you think I'd let you—marry—a cripple, a lump of stone?" she demanded, and something in the buoyant tone made him laugh unreasonably.

"I think — you've got to," he answered, his head swimming a bit.

"Ah, but that's where you're wrong," and she shook her finger at him triumphantly. "I'm — going — to — get — well."

"I knew it all along," the man said, smiling.

"That's a lie!" she announced, so prettily, in the soft, buoyant voice, that he laughed with sheer pleasure. "You never knew. Do you know where I've been?"

"In Germany."

"I haven't been in Germany a minute." The bright face grew grave and again the quick, rainbow tears flashed. "You never heard," she said. "Uncle Ted died, the day before we were to sail." She stopped a moment. "It left me alone and — and pretty desperate. I — I almost telegraphed you."

"*Why* didn't you?" he groaned.

"Because — what I said. I wouldn't sacrifice you." She paid no attention to the look in his eyes. "Robin was going to my place in Georgia — I told you I had a place? My father's old shooting-box. I'd arranged for him to do that. With some people who needed it. So — I went too. I took two trained nurses and some old souls — old sick people. Yes, I did. Wasn't it queer of me? I'm always sorrier for old people than for children. They realize, the old people. So I scraped up a few astonished old parties, and they groaned and wheezed and found fault, but had a wonderful winter. The first time I was ever any good to anybody in my life. I thought I might as well do one job before I petrified. And all winter Robin was talking about that boneologist from France who had been in Forest Gate, and whom I wouldn't see. Till at last he got me inspired, and I said I'd go to France and see him. And I've just been. And he says —" suddenly the bright, changing face was buried in her hands and she was sobbing as if her heart would break.

McBirney's pulse stopped; he was terrified. "What?" he demanded. "Never mind what he said, dear. I'll take care of you. Don't trouble, my own —" And then again the sunshine flashed through the storm and she looked up, all tears and laughter.

"He said I'd get well," she threw at him. "In time. With care. And if you don't understand that I've got to cry when I'm glad, then we can never be happy together."

"I'll get to understand," he promised, with a thrill as he thought how the lesson would be learned. And went on: "There's another conundrum. Of course—that man—he's not on earth—but how did you—kill him?"

The girl looked bewildered a moment. "Who? Oh! Alec. My dear—" and she slid her hand into his as if they had lived together for years—"the most glorious thing—he jilted me. He eloped with Natalie Minturn—the California girl—the heiress. She had"—the girl laughed again—"more money than I. And unimpeachable bones. She's a nice thing," she went on regretfully. "I'm afraid she's too good for Alec. But she liked him; I hope she'll go on liking him. It was a great thing for me to get jilted. Any more questions in the Catechism? Will the High-Mightiness take me now? Or have I got to beg and explain a little more?"

"You're a very untruthful character," said "the High-Mightiness" unsteadily. "It wasn't I who hid away, and turned last winter into hell for a well-meaning parson. Will—I take you? Come."

Again eternal things brooded over the bright, quiet garden and the larkspur spires swayed unnoticed and the bees droned casually about them and dived into deep cups of the lilies, and peace and sunshine and lovely things growing were everywhere. But the two did not notice.

After a time: "What about Halarkenden?" asked the man, holding a slim hand tight as if he held to a life-preserver.

"That's the last question in the Catechism," said Hope Stuart. "And the answer is the longest. One of your letters did it."

"One of my letters?"

"Just the other day. I went to Forest Gate, as soon as I came home from France—to tell Robin that I was going to get well. I was in the garden. With—I hate to tell you—but with—all your letters." The man flushed. "And—and Robin came and—and I talked a little to him about you, and then, to show him what you were like, I read him — some."

"You did?" McBirney looked troubled.

"Oh, I selected. I read about the boy, Theodore — 'the Gift.'"

Then she went on to tell how, as she sat in a deep chair at the end of a long pergola where small, juicy leaves of Dorothy Perkins rose-vines and of crimson ramblers made a green May mist over the line of arches, Halarkenden had come down under them to her.

"I believe I shall never be in a garden without expecting to see him stalk down a path," she said. She told him how she had read to him about the boy Theodore with his charm and his naughtiness and his Scotch name. How there had been no word from Robert Halarkenden when she finished, and how, suddenly, she had been aware of a quality in the silence which startled her, and she had looked up sharply. How, as she looked, the high-featured, lean, grave face was transformed with a color which she had never seen there before, a painful, slow-coming color; how the muscles about his mouth were twisting. How she had cried out, frightened, and Robert Halarkenden, who had not fought with the beasts for noth-ing, had controlled himself once again and, after a moment, had spoken steadily. "It was the boy's name, lassie," he had said. "He comes of folk whom I knew — back home." How at that, with his big clippers in his hand, he had turned quietly and gone working again among his flowers.

"But is that all?" demanded McBirney, interested. "Didn't he tell you any more? Could Theodore be any kin to him, do you suppose? It would be wonderful to have a man like that who took an interest. I'll write the young devil. He's been away all winter, but he should be back by now. I wonder just where he is."

And with that, as cues are taken on the stage, there was a scurry-ing down the gravel and out of the sunshine a bare-headed, tall lad was leaping toward them.

"By all that's uncanny!" gasped McBirney.

"Yes, me," agreed the apparition. "I trailed you. Why" — he inter-rupted himself — "didn't you get my telephones? Why, somebody took the message—twice. Cost three dollars—had to pawn stuff to pay it. Then I trailed you. The rector had your address. We're going to Scotland bang off and I had to see you. We're sailing from Boston. To-morrow."

"Who's 'we'?" demanded McBirney.

"My family and—oh gosh, you don't know!" He threw back his handsome head and broke into a great shout of young laughter. With that he whirled and flung out an arm. "There he comes. My family." The pride and joy in the boy's voice were so charged with years of loneliness past that the two who listened felt an answering thrill.

They looked. Down the gravel, through the sunshine, strayed, between flower borders, a gaunt and grizzled man who bent, here and there, over a blossom, and touched it with tender, wise fingers and gazed this way and that, scrutinizing, absorbed, across the masses of living color.

"I told you," the girl said, as if out of a dream, and her arm, too, was stretched and her hand pointed out the figure to her lover. "I told you there never would be a garden but he would be in it. It's Robin."

SATURDAY NIGHT LATE.
WARCHESTER,
St. Andrew's Parish House.

There wasn't time to leave you a note even. I barely caught the train. Dick was to tell you. I wonder if he got it straight. He motored me to the station, early this morning—a thousand years ago. You see the rector suddenly wired for me to come back for over Sunday. It's Sunday morning now—at least by the clock.

There's still such a lot to tell you. There always will be. One really can't say much in only eight or nine hours, and I don't believe we talked a minute longer. That's why I didn't want to catch trains. Well, there were other reasons too, now I go into it.

Do you know, I keep thinking of Dick Marston's face when he poked it in at the door of that summer-house yesterday on you and

"Robin" and Theodore and me. I think likely Dick's brain is sprained.

Curious, isn't it—this being knocked back into the necessity of writing letters—and so soon. But I can say anything now, can't I? It doesn't seem true, but it is—it is! When I think of that other letter, that last one, and all the months that I didn't know even where you were! And now here's the world transfigured. It *is* true, isn't it? I won't wake up into that awful emptiness again? So many times I've done that. I'd made up my mind nothing was any use. I told Dick, just before we started on the motor trip. The stellar system had gone to pieces. But to-night I tore up the letter I'd got ready to send to the rector. All those preparations, and then to walk down a gravel path into heaven. It isn't the slightest trouble for you to rebuild people's worlds, is it? As for instance, Theodore's. I must tell you that some incoherences have come in from that Gift of God, by way of the pilot, after they'd sailed. Mostly regarding Cousin Robin. Even that has worked out. And there's Halarkenden—mustn't I say McGregor, though?—going back home to wander at large in paradise. Three new worlds you set up in half an hour. I think you said once that you'd never done anything for anybody? Well, you've begun your job; didn't I tell you it might be just around the corner? Besides "Cousin Robin," two things stuck out in Theodore's epistle; he's going to turn himself loose for the benefit of those working people in his factories, and he's going to have "The Cairns" swept and garnished for you and me when—when we get there.

This is all true. I am sitting here, writing to her. She is going to be there when I get back. I am to have her for my own, to look at and to listen to and to love. She has said that she wanted it like that—I heard her say it. Oh my dear darling, there aren't any words to tell you—you are like listening to music—you are the spirit of all the exquisite wonders that have ever been—you are the fragrant silence of shut gardens sleeping in the moonlight. What if I had missed you? What if I'd never found you? You *will* be there when I come back—you won't vanish—you *are* real? Think of the life opening out for you and me; this world now; afterwards the next. Oh my very dear, suppose you hadn't waited—suppose you'd cut into God's big pattern because some dark threads had to be woven into it! We shall look at the whole of it some day — all that mighty, living tapestry of His weaving, and we shall understand, then, and smile as we remember and know that no one can have a sense of light without the shadows. Suppose you hadn't waited? But you did wait — you did — to let me love you.

SEA-ACRES,
MONDAY, June 24th.

YOUR REVERENCE.

I can't say but three words. Don Emory is waiting to post this in town. I do just want to tell you that if you write any more letters like that I am *not* going to break the engagement. You'll get the rest of this to-morrow. I thought I'd warn you. I am, for sure, yours,

AUGUST FIRST.